TURK THE BORDER COLLIE

TURK
THE BORDER
COLLIE

Kathleen Fidler

Illustrated by Mary Dinsdale

CANONGATE · KELPIES

In
grateful memory
of
DAVID MURRAY, Senior,
of
Glenbield, Peebles,
who bred and trained
TURK
and with gratitude too
to the present kindly Murray family
at Glenbield

The author would also like to express her thanks to Laurence Henson of International Film Associates, who suggested this book and who also filmed *Flash the Sheep-Dog*.

First published 1975 by the Lutterworth Press
First published in Kelpies 1986
This impression 1993

Copyright © 1975 Kathleen Fidler

Cover illustration by Alexa Rutherford

Printed in Denmark
by Nørhaven AS Rotation

ISBN 0 86241 130 0

The publishers acknowledge the financial assistance
of the Scottish Arts Council in the
publication of this volume

CANONGATE PRESS LTD
14 FREDERICK STREET, EDINBURGH EH2 2HB

Contents

A map showing Turk's journey appears on page 153

"Surely we can take a look at Lil's puppies today, Grandpa?" Ann coaxed old David Murray. "You did promise you'd let us see them if we kept out of the byre for a day or two."

"Aye, lassie, I did, but it doesna' do to hurry Lil. She's likely to be a bit over-anxious at first about her pups. All bitches are feared any harm might come to their new-born babies."

"But she knows *us*. She knows *we* wouldn't hurt them."

David Murray pursed his lips thoughtfully but his kind weather-beaten face creased into a half-smile. "Aye, maybe she does, seeing you've all played together since you and your sister were wee bairns and she was a pup herself. Perhaps we could take a chance on it," he conceded.

"Oh, Grandpa!" Ann clasped her hands in delight. She shouted excitedly at the kitchen door, "Come on, Helen! We can see Lil's pups."

"Quietly, now, lassie, quietly! You and your sister have not to go tearing into the byre like a bull at a gate. You'll come doucely behind me and if Lil so much as growls in her throat, you go straight out again, you understand?"

"So we will, Grandpa," Ann promised.

"You can tell Helen to bring a jug of milk. If Lil doesna' resent you looking at her babies, she'll maybe welcome a drink."

9

Carrying the jug, Ann and Helen tiptoed into the byre behind David Murray. "Ye're no' to touch the pups, mind!" he cautioned them.

Lil was lying in a corner of the byre on a bed of clean straw, her puppies snuggled close to her. She raised her head at the opening of the door but her tail gave a thump of welcome at the sight of old David. She looked at the girls out of the corner of her eye, but she showed no signs of resentment when they halted a few paces away.

"How many puppies has she got?" Helen asked in a hushed whisper.

"Five. I think there are three boys among them but I havena' touched any of them yet," her grandfather told her. "We'll wait till she's got more used to us looking at them.

You can come a bit closer and pour some milk into her dish."

Lil's tail bumped up and down and she gave a lick of pride to the pups as they squirmed close to her.

"They're lovely! Shall we keep them all, Grandpa?" Helen asked.

"Mercy me, no, lassie! What would we be doing with Garry and Lil and Vick *and* five puppies rushing about the farm? We couldna' find work with the sheep for *eight* dogs!"

Helen's face fell. "Will you be selling them, then, Grandpa?"

"There are several sheep farmers along Tweedside would be glad to buy a sheep-dog from Glenbield. Our dogs have a name for being good workers and they do weel at the Sheep-Dog Trials," he said. "We'll have to wait till they're old enough to be taken from their mother and can feed themselves, though, so you'll be able to watch them for three or four months."

Ann looked forlorn. "Only three months! Won't you be keeping *any* of them, Grandpa?"

David Murray smiled his slow, kind smile. "Weel, perhaps one of them. Your father could be doing with another dog in training now the flocks are growing. And maybe I'd like to be at the training of a dog again for the Sheep-Dog Trials." His eyes twinkled.

Old David Murray had trained many prize-winning dogs in his time, among them more than one Scottish champion. His kindness and patience with his dogs were renowned all over the Border country and the Glenbield breed of sheep-dogs was sought after by many a sheep farmer.

"Which puppy will you choose, Grandpa?" Helen asked.

"It's a bit early to be choosing yet, my lass."

"That looks a bonnie wee pup," Ann said, pointing to one of the litter, a fat little ball of black and white fur.

"Aye, he's got nice markings, that one," David Murray agreed.

"Just look at the white flash up from his nose over his head to the white ruff round his neck! Oh, will you keep him, Grandpa?" Helen asked.

"Weel, I might at that," he nodded. "But that pup looks a good one too." He pointed to another puppy.

"Oh no, Grandpa! Keep our one!" Ann urged him. "Just look at him pushing the other pups out of his way so he can get his feed from his mother, the little Turk!"

Helen clapped her hands. "That's what we could call him, *Turk*. Let's keep that one and call him Turk, Grandpa."

"Aye, it's a good short name for a sheep-dog," her grandfather approved. "A fancy name like some you get in dog shows is no use for a sheep-dog. A quick, sharp one is best that he can soon learn."

"Then you'll keep him, Grandpa?" Ann begged.

Grandfather Murray looked indulgently at his two grand-daughters. He was very fond of them both and secretly very pleased that they took such an interest in his dogs but he could not resist teasing them in his quiet way. "Yes, weel, maybe I could keep that one, but the other one has a wee bit more intelligent look, perhaps, don't you think?" He pretended to be undecided.

"Oh, but, Grandpa, Turk is *beautiful*," Ann protested.

Her grandfather chuckled. "I'll grant you that, my lass, but remember it's not just good looks that make a good sheep-dog. He needs intelligence like Garry."

Garry was nearly two years old and already beginning to show signs of being a possible future champion.

"I'm sure Turk'll be just as intelligent as Garry," Ann said stoutly.

"All right, then. As a favour to you both I'll keep him." David Murray's eyes twinkled. He had already made up his mind to keep Turk.

Before long Turk and the rest of Lil's litter were making

their first unsteady steps in the farmyard and it was safe for
the little girls to handle them without upsetting Lil. She
watched her pups indulgently as they tumbled over one
another in play, but when they got too excited she nosed
them all back again into the security of the byre. Once they
were able to run freely about the farmyard David Murray
began to supplement their food with minced meat and vege-
tables and plenty of gravy. Soon they recognised the clatter
of the spoon on the dish and came running towards him, their
tongues licking in and out and their little jaws dribbling with
anticipation. Turk was usually the leader. Once her puppies
began to fend well for themselves Lil gradually lost interest
in feeding them. She would rise and shake them away from
her and stalk out of the byre and make for the little hill above
the farm. There she sniffed the air and pointed her nose towards the surrounding hills.

"Aye. Lil's longing to be out after the sheep again," old
David remarked to his son, also called David. "The pups are
old enough to be separated from her now." So the little family
was split up and four of the pups went to their new farm
homes but Turk stayed at Glenbield.

Glenbield was tucked away in a fold of the hills just north
of the pleasant market town of Peebles in the Southern up-
lands of Scotland. All around were the rolling green moun-
tains, dotted with sheep, and seamed with many tinkling
streams rushing down to join the Tweed, wide and swift at
Peebles. Behind Venlaw Castle the road to the farm climbed
a steep stony track till one looked down from a dizzy height
on to the Soonhope Water, a silver thread far below. At inter-
vals along the road were gates which those coming and going
to and from the farm must open to pass through, and then
close again behind them. It was important to remember to
close the gates or the sheep might stray into forbidden
pastures. From the cliff-like height the track took a sudden

plunge downward, and there, as if held by a great hand in the hollow of the hills, nestled the farm, snug and comely, plumes of smoke rising from its kitchen chimney. There was always a good smell of baking at the farm, for young Mrs

David Murray, daughter-in-law to old David, was a powerful hand with the scones and oatcakes. There was always a warm welcome to visitors from the happy family that dwelt there. The farm and its family were part of the peace and gentleness of those smooth green hills.

As soon as Turk was old enough to understand he was taught to answer to his name. When he was little more than a fat football of black and white wool he would come racing across to old David whenever he called him. There was always a pat on the head for an obedient dog and the occasional titbit. The next thing Turk had to learn was to come to heel. David first took him on a leash for a walk along the farm road. The old man always took his shepherd's stick with the crooked handle but he would have scorned to use it on any of his dogs. It was just there to indicate his orders, for all David Murray's dogs were trained by kindness. He cried, "Come ahint!" and indicated with his stick a place immediately behind him. Whenever Turk tried to pass in front of him on either side, David waved his stick before him. Turk darted from one side to the other but the stick was always there. At last he gave up trying to pass it and trotted meekly behind his master, but he cast longing eyes over the hillside and sniffed the scent of rabbits and now and again he strained at the leash.

Ann often joined her grandfather on these training walks. "Are you pleased with Turk? Is he doing well?" she asked him one day.

"No' badly!" her grandfather answered, pausing to light his pipe. "He'd do better if he wasna' so interested in the rabbits. He's no' quite as biddable as Garry was but once he's introduced to the sheep, maybe his liking for the rabbits 'll fade."

"When will you let him drive the sheep?" Ann asked.

"Not yet, Ann. He's got to learn to follow me without the

leash first and to stop at a word of command and come back to me when I whistle for him. But first we'll teach him to crouch down when he's told. You can help with that if you like."

Ann was delighted. "Show me how, Grandpa."

"I keep the leash on him, then I press downward on his collar." Gently David forced the little dog into a crouching position, saying in a loud voice as he did so, "Down!" He repeated the drill several times, then handed the leash to Ann. "Now you have a go."

At first Turk looked appealingly to David Murray when he felt the lighter pressure of the girl's hand but David said sternly, "Down, Turk! Down!" The dog sank obediently to the ground.

"Soon we'll have no need to press his head and neck. He'll crouch of his own accord at the word 'Down!'" David predicted.

It only took a few lessons of ten minutes each day till Turk learned to crouch obediently at the word of command.

"Aye, he's got brains and sense, that one," David said, well pleased. "Now he'll be ready for the ducks."

"The ducks, Grandpa?" Ann laughed.

"Yes, he must learn to herd ducks to the pond before we try him on the sheep. We'll see then if he's got the eye."

"The eye? Why he's got two lovely hazel eyes!" Ann exclaimed.

"Maybe I should have said 'The power of the eye'," David explained. "All good sheep-dogs have it but some better than others. It's the power to hold the sheep in one place just by staring at them. If he can do it with ducks then he'll do it later with sheep. Come along, we'll give him a try."

They went down to the duck-pond near the stream, Turk following obediently now without the leash. The ducks were waddling in a procession across the strip of green meadow towards the pond. The sight of them was too much for Turk. He rushed at them and the ducks scattered, angrily quacking. "Down, Turk! Down!" David Murray shouted.

At first Turk took a rebellious leap towards the ducks but stopped in his stride and looked back at David. Then he crouched down, keeping his eye on the ducks all the time. They huddled into a corner by the fence, quacking indignantly but staring back at Turk as if hypnotised by his eye, only moving nervously on their flat, webbed feet. Turk remained motionless, his head raised, watching them.

"Good dog, Turk! You've got the eye all right," David Murray chuckled. Though Turk thumped his tail, happy at the praise, he did not stir from his position nor take his baleful eye off the ducks.

"The ducks just daren't stir!" Ann exclaimed.

"No. He's got them penned up in the corner, but we'll let him have his bit of fun." Grandfather Murray called, "Come awa', Turk!"

Surprised and reluctant Turk rose and came towards David Murray. As if released from a spell the ducks began to move towards the pond, fluttering their wings and shoving each other in their hurry to reach the safety of the water.

"Go ahint, Turk! Go ahint!" David Murray urged the dog, pointing to the ducks. Turk rushed behind the stragglers who waddled from him in a panic. "Quietly now, Turk! Don't frighten them. Easy now!" Murray commanded. Turk seemed to understand, stopped his headlong rush and ran back and forth behind the ducks. Propelled by fear the ducks fled from him to the water. Only when they were safely afloat did they turn and face him again and unite in quacks of defiance. Even then Turk might have followed them into the water but a word from David Murray stopped him.

"Down, Turk! Down! You've done weel."

Turk wagged his tail in delight at the praise and barked back at the ducks.

"Quiet, Turk! Good sheep-dogs shouldna' bark overmuch," David told him. Turk gave one protesting "Wuff!" and was silent.

"What about trying him with driving the sheep now, Grandpa?" Ann asked.

"No' yet, Ann. His legs are far ower short yet. He couldna' run fast enough to get round the flock and he might get discouraged. No, we'll keep him at the ducks a wee while yet and wait till he's about nine months old before we put him to the sheep."

"Is he doing as well as Garry did?"

"He was right quick, was Garry. He'll make a champion some day."

"But what about Turk? Will he make a champion too?" Ann persisted.

"We'll see, lassie, we'll see in time. He's not quite so quick learning to obey, but he's young yet." David Murray saw the disappointed look in his grand-daughter's eye. He knew Turk was her favourite so he consoled her by saying, "Oh, Turk's good too, don't mistake me. There's something about Turk too that's a bit different. He's more affectionate and stays by me."

"Father says Garry obeys other people's commands too, but Turk won't listen to anyone but you."

"He could be right there," old David said with a hint of a pleased smile. Turk was beginning to be his special dog too. "But there are other things we must teach Turk. He must learn to stand guard over things and mind them. A good sheep-dog should be a good watch-dog too. I'll put something on the ground and tell him to watch it. Now, what shall it be?"

"It had better be something belonging to you, Grandpa. He's more likely to watch it then," Ann said with insight.

The old man put his cap on the ground. "Down, Turk! Watch it!" he ordered. Turk obediently crouched and fixed his eye on the cap as though it might run away. David moved towards the other side of the field. Turk made to follow him but David pointed sternly at the cap and repeated the command, "Down! Watch it!" Turk looked from the cap to his master and back again as if uncertain where his duty lay but David's stern finger still pointed at the cap. Turk almost gave a sigh but settled down beside the cap, keeping his eye on it.

Before long David called, "Bring it to me!" and pointed to the cap. For a moment Turk did not quite know what to do but he and David had long had a game where David threw sticks and Turk brought them back to him. He recognised the words of command and with a sharp bark of delight he seized the cap and brought it triumphantly to David. Every day afterwards David gave him something of his own to guard, sometimes his scarf, once even his cherished pipe. Even if Ann or Helen put down something belonging to their grandfather, such as his coat or stick, and told the dog to watch it, Turk knew by scent that it belonged to his master and he would mount guard over it jealously.

One day while her grandfather was reading his paper after dinner Ann lifted his 'deer-stalker' checked hat from its peg. This was the one he wore at the Friday market in Peebles. She tiptoed outside, seized something from the farm-yard, thrust it under the hat and set it down on the cobble-stones and called to Turk, "Watch it, Turk!"

Turk crept in a crouching position towards the hat, fixed his eyes on it as if to mesmerise it and uttered a low growl. Ann called her grandfather out into the yard. Turk gave a quick "Wuff!" but he did not move from his position.

"Mercy me! How did the rascal get my best hat?" David exclaimed. "Come away, Turk!" Turk did not stir. He crawled nearer to the hat, never moving his eyes from it. Then, surprisingly, the hat began to move of its own accord! Growling low in his throat Turk followed it. The hat stopped! Turk stopped too, crouching behind it. David could hardly believe his eyes.

"What, in the name of fortune —" he began, then the hat began to move again. Turk growled and crawled after it.

"Hi, Turk, bring it to me!" David cried.

Turk made one bound and seized the hat. From beneath it fluttered a frightened young duckling which made straight for the pond.

"That's you, Ann, you young besom!" Grandpa exclaimed as he retrieved his cherished hat. "Small wonder that Turk 'set' the hat the way he did! He knew weel that the hat had no business to be moving of itself. He was using the power of the eye on the hat!" Grandpa joined in the laugh against himself. "Weel done, Turk!" He patted the dog.

From that day on, though, Turk watched David Murray's hat with suspicion whenever he went to the Friday market. For fun David would set it down on a bench and tell Turk to watch it. Turk never stirred from it and growled warningly if any other farmer offered to touch it. Soon all David's possessions belonged to Turk too.

"I'm not sure *I* don't belong to Turk as weel," David Murray laughed. The relationship between them grew even closer. If David owned the dog, the dog owned David too. Turk had eyes and ears for no one else.

During the next year David Murray began to train Turk to drive the sheep. As soon as his legs were big and strong enough he had to learn to "make a cast"; that is, to run fast round a flock and come up well behind them. From this position the dog had to drive the sheep up or down a hill and to head off stragglers or disobedient sheep. David started with a group of half a dozen sheep which were enough for the young dog to handle, then he gradually increased the size of the flock as Turk grew more experienced. Now came the time to work him with the flocks on the hills along with Garry. At first Garry gave a sniff of disapproval and a wuff of disgust when he found Turk was to be included in the work force. Garry answered, too, to commands from David Murray's son, the younger David Murray, the father of Helen and Ann, but Turk always looked to old David Murray for his orders and to no one else.

The two men watched Turk and Garry make a cast round the flock to bring them down the hill.

"Turk's got a fine turn of speed. That was a near perfect cast he made round the flock just now," young David said. "Even Garry was no quicker off his mark."

"Oh, aye, Turk's speedy enough but he's no' as steady as Garry. Watch what happens when I whistle the dogs to stop." David Murray blew a long blast on his whistle. At once

Garry stopped dead in his tracks and crouched down, never taking his eyes off the sheep. Turk did not take his eyes off the sheep either but he went on for a yard or two before crouching down, as if determined to get in front of Garry. Garry was aware of this and he growled low in his throat as though reproving Turk.

"Turk's no' quite as biddable as Garry," old David remarked.

"I wouldna' say that, Father. I think he's just that bit jealous of Garry and he feels he must be a bit ahead of Garry to please *you*."

"Aye, weel, he'll please me better by obeying promptly."

"Och, he's only a young dog yet and ower eager. You'll see he'll do you credit when it comes to the Sheep-Dog Trials."

Old David whistled the dogs on with two sharp quick blasts on his whistle and the flock continued downhill.

"You'll be entering Turk for the Trials?" his son asked.

The old man looked undecided. "I canna just make up my mind. He lacks Garry's experience and steadiness yet."

"Oh, that'll come," young David said easily. "Turk always does better when he's on his own with you. He can't bear to share you with another dog, Dad. You mean an awful lot to Turk."

It was true that Turk hung on every word and sign from old David Murray. A word of displeasure from the old man and Turk would slink away behind him with drooping ears and his tail between his legs. At a word of praise his eyes brightened, his ears came up and his tail bashed wildly from side to side. He was old David Murray's dog completely, body and soul. He followed him everywhere about the farm and when David took a nap in his chair, the dog lay down at his feet and seemed to sleep too, but at the least movement of his master a wary eye would open and Turk's head lift from his paws.

"I think Turk owns *you*, Dad," young David told his father with a laugh.

The time came round for the Sheep-Dog Trials to be held at Peebles. The girls were eager that Turk should make his first appearance at them but their grandfather was not so enthusiastic.

"You *will* enter Turk, won't you, Grandpa?" Ann pleaded.

"I doubt if he's really ready for a competition yet but perhaps I'll try him out in a class for young dogs. It'll be an experience for him," David conceded at last.

From then on Turk was constantly kept in training. He

had already learned to come round in a great arc behind the sheep, to crouch on his stomach, keeping his eye on them, then in short rushes to drive them down the hill before him. Next he learned to drive the flock through a gate. He also learned to drive the sheep into a pen while David Murray held the gate of it open. Next he had to learn to drive the flock into groups as David Murray required. Sometimes a sheep had to be taken out of the flock for special treatment for some injury or ailment. It was Turk's job to "single out" the sheep old David pointed out to him. This was the hardest thing of all to do for it often seemed as if the single sheep was trying to avoid capture. It hid among other sheep, danced about and twisted in and out of the flock. Difficult though the task was, to Turk, David's command was law. He plunged in and out of the flock till he had separated his sheep. David always gave him praise when he had accomplished it, sometimes tempered with a word of warning.

"Weel done, Turk! Weel done, lad! But you must learn to do it quietly and not set the flock half-demented."

Turk always knew when he had done specially well, for then David dived into his pocket and brought out *one* chocolate drop by way of reward.

"Why, Grandpa, you've given me *four* chocolate drops and you've only given Turk *one*," Ann exclaimed one day. "Shall I share mine with him?"

"No, my lass, *you're* not in training. Turk is. I don't want to give him ower many chocolate drops and ruin his wind. That dog's got to run hard. Besides, he's learned that a chocolate drop is only for when he's done his very best, so I don't want you to be giving him chocolate drops all round the clock and spoiling him for his work."

Ann was a sensible girl. She knew how kind her grand-father was to his animals. If he thought it was better that Turk should not be pampered, then he was right. He had trained Garry and Garry had carried off several prizes at Sheep-Dog Trials.

"Do you think Turk will do better than Garry at the Sheep-Dog Trials?" she asked.

Her grandfather smiled, but he shook his head. "Turk may do well enough in his own class but he wouldn't outshine Garry in an open competition. I shall enter Garry for the Open event. He's got just that bit more sense than Turk when it comes to putting sheep into a pen. He does it with less fuss."

Ann looked a bit downcast. She would have liked to see her favourite entered for the Open competition, but she knew the wisdom of her grandfather's choice. Nevertheless she hugged Turk to her and said challengingly, "Garry may have more sense, Turk, but you are more *beautiful*."

"Aye, Turk's beautiful, right enough," David Murray agreed. "But it's no' a beauty competition he's entering for."

"Some day, Turk, *you'll* outshine Garry and everyone will know about it then."

"There's no harm in hoping, lassie, no harm at all," David Murray smiled at her.

· When the day of the Sheep-Dog Trials dawned the whole Murray family rose with the lark on that lovely June morning. The farm animals had all been fed and penned before the family left for the Trials. Mrs Murray had the breakfast on the table very early and was busy making up the picnic lunch they would take with them. The girls helped their grandfather to groom the dogs. Helen took over Garry and Ann groomed Turk. David Murray had seen that the dogs were well-washed the night before in the stream at the foot of the valley. Now Garry and Turk had to stand still, obedient and patient, at the whole performance of brushing and combing them till their coats shone like spun silk and the "feathers" on their legs and chests stood out.

"I must say there'll not be a better groomed pair anywhere at the Trials," David Murray praised his grand-daughters' handiwork.

"There isn't a more handsome dog than Turk," Ann said proudly.

"Remember, handsome is as handsome does!" Helen quoted the old proverb. If Turk was Ann's favourite, then Garry was Helen's.

At last they were all ready to go in the Landrover to the Trials, Mrs Murray and the girls in gay summery dresses and David Murray and his son in their Sunday suits, for this was a special occasion among the sheep farmers in the south of Scotland when all the families met.

The Sheep-Dog Trials were being held in the Hay Lodge Park at Peebles. Here a long green meadow fringed by trees sloped eastward. Below it, a short distance away, the River Tweed wound its rushing, silvery way towards the town. It was an ideal place for the Trials: plenty of room for the dogs, leafy shade for the waiting sheep and room alongside the course for the many cars that would bring the sheep farmers and their wives and families. Greetings and hearty handshakes were exchanged all round. The farmers, in their good tweed suits and carrying their long, crooked sticks, gathered in little groups and discussed the fat-stock prices of sheep and cattle. Their wives swapped country gossip and family news and admired new additions to families since the last Sheep-Dog Trials. The dogs stood or sat close beside their owners, the young dogs panting a little, their tongues licking in and out. The older dogs seemed unconcerned, even a bit bored, as if to say "We've seen all this before", but now and again they cast sideways glances at their rivals.

Garry and Turk sat at the feet of Grandfather Murray and the girls. Garry was quiet and sedate but Turk's head turned here and there, watching this strange new scene. Every now and again he thrust his muzzle into old David's hand as if seeking confidence. Ann stroked the dog's long, shining hair with pride. "You're beautiful, Turk, just beautiful," she murmured. People passing by smiled at the little girl's delight in her dog. One man in particular walked past two or three times and looked at the dogs with interest. As time wore on to eleven o'clock the little groups of chatting friends broke up and they took positions along the rope which bounded the Trials' field, so they could get a good view of the competing dogs.

Turk's turn came early in the proceedings when the event for young dogs took place. He followed at the heels of David Murray to the field and stood beside him at the starting post, looking up at the old man and waiting for the word of command. He looked slightly puzzled at the crowds of people lining the rope and his eye searched the field for the flock of sheep. There, four hundred yards away, where the field sloped upward to a small hillock, a group of sheep was being assembled by the shepherds and their dogs. Only six sheep! Turk looked surprised. He was used to dealing with far bigger numbers. He looked up at David. Why were they waiting? Did David want him to gather those sheep or not?

Just then the judge's whistle shrilled to mark the start of the event. The time-keepers' stop-watches clicked. David Murray had just ten minutes to direct Turk through the various tests. He wasted no time. He pointed to the sheep. "Awa', Turk!" he cried. Turk went away like an arrow to the right hand, curved round and came in behind the little flock.

"A wonderful outrun, that!" one farmer exclaimed. "My! What a turn of speed! Old David Murray's bred another champion there."

"Aye, but the dog's got to do other things besides run," his friend reminded him.

A loud whistle from David halted Turk behind the little flock which was edging nervously downhill. Turk crouched behind the sheep, never taking his eyes off them. Two quieter whistles in quick succession told Turk he could begin moving the sheep again. He came in closer behind them and began running back and forth, forcing a sheep which was trying to break away, to rejoin the others. Cleverly he kept the six sheep in a compact group as they began to scamper before him down the hill. Time and again David Murray blew the long blast on his whistle that made Turk crouch suddenly like a lion about to spring. Then the six sheep stopped running and dawdled to a halt to turn and face Turk again. Turk glared at them from his rigid position and they stayed still as if mesmerised.

"That dog's got the power of the eye right enough," a spectator commented. "He's got those sheep under control."

Ann whispered to her father, "Turk's doing well, isn't he?"

"No' badly. No' badly," her father agreed. "He's learned to gather sheep all right."

At David Murray's double short whistle Turk brought the

little flock straight down the field and through the gate set mid-way across the course.

"Turk's lost no time there, anyway," young David Murray said.

The next test was to drive the sheep diagonally through a gate on the left, then to bring them across the course and through another gate on the right. Old David gave a series of whistled instructions to Turk to bundle his sheep together on the left. Just then one sheep began to be frisky and to bound

away from the others. Turk went after it to round it up. At first it faced him defiantly and stamped its feet, but at Turk's stony stare it trotted back to the others. Alas, by then they were also scattering. Turk had a busy couple of minutes rounding them up and re-grouping them again in a bunch to take them through the next gate.

"Turk's lost time there a bit," young David said, consulting his watch anxiously.

"He *did* get the sheep through, though," Ann said, defending her pet.

Turk took the sheep across the field to the right-hand gate. Here again the disobedient sheep gave trouble. She tried to run round the gate instead of through it. Turk went after her at once. The sheep eluded him and went through the gate the wrong way.

"Oh, I could shake that silly sheep!" Ann cried in exasperation.

A few seconds later, however, Turk had sorted out the wrongdoer and brought her through the gate the proper way after the others.

"Aye, Turk's been a bit unlucky with that one," her father commented, "but he's got the sheep through the three gates now."

Turk brought the sheep down towards his master who stood in a marked ring twenty yards across. After some slight hustling Turk got them all into the ring. His next task was to separate the little flock into two and four. David Murray indicated with his stick how he wished the flock to be divided. Turk went among the sheep, crouching before two of them and eyeing them till he had got them on the far side of the ring.

"Turk did that very neatly," Helen declared.

The next test was a more exacting one. Turk had to bring the sheep from the shedding ring and into a six-foot square pen having a gate on one side. David Murray went to the gate which was secured by a rope six feet long. He held the gate open at the full stretch of the rope and called to Turk, "Come on!" and pointed with his stick to the pen.

Turk had had a lot of practice at penning sheep. Behind the little flock he ran, urging them towards the pen. As though they did not wish to be penned the sheep began to run this way and that.

"Oh, dear! They're going to scatter!" Ann wailed.

As fast as the sheep moved, Turk moved even faster. He crouched and ran and crouched and ran at old David's whistle till he had got all the sheep in a bunch again. This time, though, they were facing away from the pen instead of towards it.

"Time's going on!" young David said anxiously, consulting his watch again.

Crouching here and there and glaring at the sheep, Turk wore them round towards the open gate of the pen. Old David Murray was still holding the gate open at the full stretch of the rope. "Come on, now, Turk! You've got them now," he encouraged the dog. Round behind the six sheep Turk ran, to and fro, edging them nearer to the open gate. At last the foremost sheep reluctantly entered the pen and the others followed on his heels. Quickly and thankfully David Murray swung the gate to close it and the six sheep were safely penned inside. David knew he was running out of time, however. Only four minutes remained now for the final test of singling out one marked sheep from the others. No sooner had he closed the gate than he opened it quickly again.

"Bring them out, Turk! Bring them to me!" he cried as he strode towards the shedding ring.

The sheep were glad to get out of the pen and Turk lost no time in bundling them across to the shedding ring. As soon as Turk had got them neatly inside the ring David pointed with his stick to one sheep marked with a blue ribbon round its neck. "That one, Turk!"

"That's the cheeky sheep that defied Turk before," Ann said gloomily.

Turk had had plenty of practice at singling out sheep. Perhaps, too, he felt that this sheep must be disciplined and he was eager to show his power over it. He went for it at once and though the sheep dodged this way and that and tried to hide behind the other sheep, it could not escape Turk. The dog was behind it all the time till he had it divided from the other sheep. Then the ribboned sheep turned and faced him and made a determined leap to try to rejoin the others but Turk was too quick for it. He crouched instantly before the sheep and cowed it with the power of his eye. Then, foot by foot, yard by yard, he "wore" the sheep backwards towards David Murray. When the sheep was at David's feet the test was over. Turk had successfully singled out his sheep. The judge's whistle blew. Turk's trial was over.

Young David had out his watch again. "Just within the time by less than half a minute!" he announced. "Phew! That was a close thing!"

Old David was mopping his brow too but he did not forget to pat Turk and to say, "Weel done! Good lad, Turk!" Turk knew he had pleased his master and gave one short sharp "Wuff!" of delight.

Ann ran to meet her grandfather and the dog as they came off the field. "Oh, Grandpa! Didn't Turk do well?" she cried as she hugged the dog with delight.

"No' badly, though he took his time about it," David Murray replied. "You can give him that chocolate drop you're hoarding in your pocket for him, my lassie," he chuckled.

Neither of them noticed the stranger who was watching them from a short distance away and who was smiling at them.

It was not long before it was Garry's turn in the Open event for older dogs. Once more old David Murray took the field with the dog he had trained. This time it was Helen's turn to watch anxiously. Turk watched too, but with a jealous eye. He and Garry got on well in the sheep pastures and the farm-yard but Turk did not like to see David give all his attention to Garry as he was doing now. Ann knew the dog was restive and she held him by the collar and stroked and patted him till he sat down beside her. All the same, he never took his eyes off her grandfather.

Garry gave a wonderful performance. He had not the same sheep that Turk had had and perhaps he was lucky in having more docile ones, but Garry was clever at handling sheep without fuss. He had a quiet determined way which even seemed to give the sheep confidence. They gave little difficulty as he drove them through the gates and though they backed away from the pen, Garry soon had them marshalled inside. He finished his singling test with three minutes to spare.

"A near perfect performance," young David declared, delighted. His father was well-pleased too and came off the course with a smile on his gentle old face.

When the judges gave their decisions later, to Ann's joy, Turk took the prize in his section, but the silver cup for the best performance in the Open event went to Garry. With pride old David Murray led up each dog in turn when he went to receive the prizes. There was loud applause for him for he was respected over the whole countryside for the wonderful training he gave his sheep-dogs, even in his old age.

"Ye've no' lost your touch wi' the dogs, Davie," an old acquaintance hailed him. "That's a good pair ye put through their paces the day, but yon Garry's a fair stunner! Of course the young one has no' had the same experience yet but I doubt if he'll ever be quite as good as Garry."

"Ye're maybe right," David Murray admitted. "Garry's a steadier dog in the field."

Ann hugged Turk closer. "Garry may be steadier but you have something no other dog has," she whispered to him. "There'll be something you'll be better at, I know. Garry won't always outshine you."

2

The stranger who had been watching the dogs at the trials
and who seemed to have a special interest in Garry and Turk
came up to David Murray and spoke quietly with him.
Young David Murray joined them. After a short conversation
young David said, "Yes, by all means come and see us at
Glenbield tomorrow. We can talk about the matter of the
dog then."

Ann's heart sank like a stone. Was the stranger coming to
buy one of the dogs? If so, which one? Garry was the more
experienced dog with the sheep and she knew her father
would prefer to keep him, but surely, surely, her grandfather
would never part with Turk who loved him so much.

That night Ann lay awake a long time, miserably wondering if Turk was to be sold. She had not told Helen her fears and Helen was sound asleep in her bed. "If Grandpa parts with Turk he'll be downright unhappy and if he parts with Garry then Helen will be upset," she told herself, and the tears fell. At last she fell asleep. She was wakened in the morning by her mother shaking her shoulder.

"Come on! Get up, sleepy-head! I'm hurrying on the breakfast. We're expecting visitors this morning."

All Ann's fears came crowding on her again. "I know!" she said gloomily.

"Don't tell me you've got the second sight!" her mother laughed. The sight of Ann's woebegone face stopped her. "Why, I thought you liked visitors?"

"Some visitors," Ann replied, pursing her lips.

Mrs Murray thought this was perhaps some private childish grief that would soon blow over. "Well, come along, my lassie! I've little time to get the breakfast things washed and put by and the coffee made ready for the visitors. You could help me by dusting the parlour."

Ann ate little breakfast and Mrs Murray began to wonder if she was sickening for some ailment. Listlessly the little girl dusted the parlour, keeping an eye the while through the window on the long stony road that came down the hill to the farm tucked in a fold of the valley. At last a jeep came careering down the rough track and halted in the steep cobbled farmyard. Two strangers got out and her father went to meet them. Just as her father was bringing them into the parlour Ann felt that she could not bear to meet them and she beat a hurried retreat into the small bedroom where she and Helen slept, which gave off the parlour.

She did not mean to eavesdrop, but she did not like to come out of the bedroom among them, so she kept perfectly still so no one would guess she was there. She heard her father offer chairs to the strangers and they exchanged some remarks about the weather and the Sheep-Dog Trials.

"Your dogs did very well," one of the strangers remarked. He was the man that Ann had seen talking to her father and grandfather at the Trials.

"No' badly!" her father admitted with evident pride.

"They're *beautiful* dogs," the stranger continued. "One of them would just suit the purpose I mentioned to you yesterday, that's if you could spare him?"

Ann's heart stood still. *Which* dog?

"My father trained both dogs. He's just bringing them in from the byre now. I'd like him to talk it over with you too," young David Murray suggested.

Grandfather Murray came in with both dogs at his heels. At a word from him they settled down beside his chair.

"What did I tell you, Ed? Aren't they just beauts?" the tall stranger asked his companion.

"You're quite right, Larry," the other man answered.

"Which one would you fancy?" Larry asked.

"I suppose a lot would depend on the temperament of the dog?" Ed suggested, turning to Grandfather Murray.

"They're both good-tempered and obedient," he told them. "If anything, Garry here is a thought more intelligent."

"Ah, but this one here is more beautiful," Larry said,

stroking Turk. "Look at the lovely flash of white going from his tufty collar over his head."

"Yes, he'd make quite a picture," Ed agreed.

"Shall we settle for this one, then?"

Ed nodded. Behind the door Ann felt as though her heart had turned to lead, but her father was saying something.

"Turk's not so biddable as Garry. I reckon Turk's a one-man dog. The only commands he obeys at once are my father's. You'd need to take my father as well."

Ann could hardly believe her ears! Surely her grandfather could never be sold along with Turk?

"Aye, Turk's a bit dour when it comes to obeying anyone else," her grandfather agreed.

"Then will you come along with him? We'd need someone to give him the proper commands," Larry asked.

"Well, I might at that. . . ." Grandfather Murray agreed.

Ann could bear no more. She flung herself into the parlour and her arms went round old David Murray. "You're not to go, Grandpa! You're not to sell Turk and leave us too!"

The old man stared at her in blank astonishment. "Easy now, lassie! What's all this about? Who's talking of selling Turk?"

"You all are!" Ann sobbed. "It's hateful!"

Larry had an understanding nature where children were concerned. He put out a hand and drew Ann towards him. "There's a mistake somewhere. Did you think we wanted to *buy* Turk and keep him for ever?"

Ann nodded dumbly.

"And your grandfather too?"

"You were asking him to leave us!" Ann found her voice at last.

"You've got it all wrong, Ann," her father told her. "These gentlemen don't want to *buy* Turk. They just want the loan of him for a few weeks to put him in a film . . . make a film star of him, if you like."

Ann's eyes opened wide. "A film star? Turk?"

"Yes, he's such a *beautiful* dog," Larry said. "You see, Ann, my friend and I make films. There's a book called *Flash the Sheep-Dog*, a story for children, and we'd like Turk to play the part of Flash."

"Turk a *real* film star?" Ann could still hardly believe it.

"Yes, and we want your grandfather to come and give the right commands to Turk."

"Would Grandpa be a film star too?" Ann sounded amazed.

"Mercy me, no, my lassie!" Grandfather answered for himself. "I'm ower old to play Cliff Richard and be a heart-throb for the teenagers, like those chaps on the telly." He turned rather anxiously to the film-makers. "Ye wouldna' be wanting *me* to appear before the camera, would ye?"

"No, no!" Ed laughed. "We'd want you to stand *behind* the camera and whistle your commands to the dog from there. There'll be a boy acting the part of Turk's owner *before* the camera."

"And you'll get Turk home every night with your Grandpa after the filming for the day's been done. And they'll both be home for good once the film has been made." Larry set Ann's heart at rest.

Ann hugged Turk in delight. "Oh, Turk! Turk! I always said you were beautiful and now everyone will know it too."

"*We* hope everyone will know it as well," Larry smiled at her.

Just then Mrs Murray and Helen came in with the coffee tray and some of her excellent buttered scones. "Ah! There you are, Ann! Will you hand round the scones while I pour out and Helen takes the cups," Mrs Murray said.

Ann handed the scones with her happiest smile to Larry.

The next three months were busy, exciting ones at Glenbield. A camera crew joined Larry and Ed, together with several actors, one of them a young boy from a London school of drama. Some of the filming was to be done in the valley of the Soonhope Water just above the farm; some on the road to the farm; some at a farm-house on the Yarrow Water and some of it at the school at Walkerburn, not far

away. The girls loved the time when the filming was done on the farm road, for when they were not at school they were able to watch Grandpa Murray standing behind the camera and giving whistled commands to Turk. The little boy from London stood in front of the camera and shouted his commands to Turk, but it was always Grandfather Murray's whistled signals that Turk obeyed. All the camera-crew grew fond of Turk and of the quiet, gentle old man. Turk might have been in danger of being spoiled but for David Murray. "Ye're no' to give him sweets and bits o' food," he told them firmly. "When ye've done wi' the dog for a film star I'll still want him to drive sheep."

During these weeks David Murray travelled round in the jeep with the film people, quietly enjoying their company and the new interest they brought with them, but always his first thought was for Turk and his welfare.

When they visited the school at Walkerburn the children were wild with excitement. "We're all on a film! We're all on a film!" they cried. There was great competition to be in the picture beside Turk but David Murray stood between them and Turk to prevent too much petting. Turk loved children and his white-bobbed tail wagged furiously with delight at all the attention they gave him.

The film story was about a London boy, Tom, who came to live in Scotland on an isolated sheep farm. Tom was miserable and lonely without his London friends till a kind farmer gave him a sheep-dog puppy for his own. His uncle helped him to train it and gradually Tom grew to understand his uncle and to settle down. When the dog won the trophy at the Sheep-Dog Trials, Tom's cup of happiness was full. Tom had many ups and downs, however, and when he attended the school he fell foul of a bully, Douglas Campbell. They had a fight. In the story the dog went to Tom's aid. It didn't quite work out like that, however, when the fight was being filmed. David Murray egged on Turk to get hold of Douglas Campbell by the trouser-leg. "Go on, Turk! Get the hold of him!" David urged, pointing at Douglas.

Just at that moment the boys swung round in the mock fight and Turk looked bewildered. Which boy? It was a bit like singling out a sheep. Obediently he dashed in, however, and seized hold of a trouser-leg. It was *Tom's!*

"Wrong boy! Wrong boy!" Ed cried. He stopped the film just as David Murray shouted, "Come awa', Turk! Come awa' to me!"

The camera crew all burst into laughter but Ed said in exasperation, "Now what do we do? We'll have to re-take all that scene."

"I canna guarantee that Turk'll go for the right boy next time, either," old David Murray said ruefully. "Ye see, both lads have been playing wi' him and giving him titbits when they weren't being filmed and he's got fond of them both."

"Maybe we can use the shots of the lads fighting and do some cutting and patching together on the film to show Turk holding *a* trouser-leg. No one watching the film will know it's the wrong trouser-leg. Both lads are wearing jeans." Larry suggested a solution.

In another scene Turk had to chase Douglas who hurriedly climbed a tree to escape the dog. Once he was up the tree Turk was to growl excitedly at the foot of the tree and to "set" Douglas with his eye as he might do a disobedient sheep. It was easy enough to get Turk to chase after Douglas. He regarded it as a kind of a game but as soon as Douglas climbed up the tree and stayed there, Turk lost interest and came away again to David Murray.

"Can't you make Turk growl at the foot of the tree and threaten Douglas?" Larry asked when they had tried to film this part of the scene three times without success.

David Murray shook his head, "Turk's been trained to set the sheep, not human beings."

"Well, we can't get a sheep to climb a tree to suit Turk," Larry declared.

"No, but we might put a duck up a tree," David Murray suggested, remembering Ann's prank with his best hat.

"But we're not filming a *duck*," Larry replied. "Besides a duck would just use its wings and flutter down again."

"Not if you put the duck in a plastic bag with just its head poking out," David Murray said. "Couldn't you film the lad looking terrified up in the tree first, and then film Turk barking and growling at the foot of the tree, using the power of his eye on the duck. You wouldn't need to photograph the duck. You did say you could cut pieces out of the film and stick it together, didn't you?"

"Grandfather Murray, we'll make a film director of you yet!" Larry cried, clapping him on the shoulder. "That's just the job!"

So a duck was brought from the farm and put in a plastic bag and placed up the tree. The duck quacked and Turk growled and snarled and set it with his eye from the foot of the tree and dared it to move, enough to satisfy all the film-makers in the world. When the shots were pieced together Larry and Ed pronounced them an absolute success. It looked as if Turk had Douglas properly treed.

At last the film-making was finished and the film crews went away and silence descended on the valley of Soonhope once more. Turk ceased to be 'Flash' and went back to driving the sheep with old David Murray, and all the family, especially the girls, felt that everything had fallen a bit flat. Autumn fell on Glenbield; the bracken turned bronze and gold, and the trees were a glory of colour; then the leaves came down to make a mottled carpet on the grass. At the foot of the steep valley the Soonhope Water rushed down in a thousand small cascades.

Winter came and ice covered the pools where the summer trout had basked; the skies grew dark with louring snow clouds and the sheep were brought down from the high hills to the better shelter of the pasture about the farm. Both old David Murray and his son, young David, were kept busy feeding chopped turnips to the flocks and bringing them water. Now and again there was an exciting job for Garry and Turk when a sheep floundered into a snow-drift and was buried by the snow till the dogs sought it out. In the farm-house the kitchen fire blazed away by day and night to dry the wet clothes of the farmers. The lamps were early lighted. Christmas and New Year festivities came and went; the days lengthened a little but the cold strengthened. Some days the snow lay so deep that the girls could not make the journey by the long rough road over the hill to school.

One such day Ann traced the frost flowers on the window with her finger. "Nothing ever seems to happen nowadays," she sighed.

"Why don't you do the sums Miss Mackenzie set us for if the road was too bad to go to school?" Helen asked.

"Done them already!" Ann told her.

"What about getting out your knitting? I thought you were making a scarf for Grandpa. It'll be summer before it's finished if you don't get on with it."

"Oh, Grandpa's got dozens of scarves! I do wish it would stop snowing and let us get to school. There'd be something to *do* there, anyway."

"What about giving me a hand with the baking?" Mrs Murray called from the kitchen. "That would give you something to do. I'll teach you how to make a sponge cake."

Just as Ann rose to her feet the telephone bell rang.

"You answer it, Ann. My hands are all floury."

Ann picked up the receiver. "Yes, yes," she answered a question with growing excitement. "Oh, yes, I do remember you. Yes, Grandpa's fine. So's Turk. They're out with the sheep just now in the sheepfank by the farm."

Helen joined her at the phone. "Who is it?" she asked in a stage whisper.

"It's Mr Larry, the film man," Ann answered, blissfully unaware that her stage whisper was being carried by phone to Glasgow. There was a chuckle at the other end of the line.

"Is your mother about then?" came the voice.

"Yes, she's in the kitchen —"

"Don't tell me! She's *baking*! I could just eat one of her scones right now!"

Mrs Murray dusted the flour off her hands and joined the girls at the telephone. "Who is it?"

"It's Mr Larry. He wants one of your scones," Ann told her.

Mrs Murray took hold of the receiver. "Mr Larry? Are you in Peebles?"

"Oh, hullo, Mrs Murray! No, I'm in Glasgow."

"But if I sent some scones to you in Glasgow they'd be stale before they reached you." Mrs Murray sounded bewildered.

Larry laughed loudly. "It wasn't really about scones I was phoning. It was to tell you that the film is finished and ready for showing now. It's to be shown in the Cosmo Cinema, Glasgow, on 21st March, a Saturday. I shall be sending an invitation for all of you, but I wanted you to know early because I know you'll have to make arrangements for someone to look after the farm animals that day."

"Oh, that's wonderful!" Mrs Murray sounded breathless. "Girls! Mr Larry is inviting us to see the film he made of Turk."

Larry could hear the excited happy exclamations from the girls.

"Oh, I want Grandpa Murray to bring Turk with him too. The audience will be children from the Glasgow schools and they'll be just thrilled to see the actual dog."

"I'll tell him that," Mrs Murray promised.

"Let's hope the snow is all over by then so it doesn't prevent you getting along the road from Glenbield."

"We shall come even if we have to dig a path through the snow right down to the main road," Mrs Murray assured him.

Luckily when the day dawned it was one of those marvellous spring days that seem to herald summer; a day to set the budding daffodils opening to the sun. Nevertheless Mrs Murray firmly clutched a furled umbrella.

"You'll no' be needing that," her husband laughed.

"It'll be raining in Glasgow. It always does and this is my best hat, I'm telling you," she declared.

Turk had been groomed till every hair looked like spun silk. The brass name-tab on his collar winked in the sun. Garry gave a reproachful bark as Turk disappeared into the Landrover with Grandfather Murray.

"Ye're to mind the farm now, Garry!" David Murray called to him.

They had started very early to drive the sixty miles to Glasgow for they had to be at the Cosmo Cinema not later than 10.30 a.m. and David Murray had to find somewhere to park the car. They were there well before 10 a.m. but already a small queue of children had formed in the entrance hall to the cinema. Larry was on the look-out for them.

"Come with me. I've got special seats for you," he told them and ushered them up the stairs to the very front row of the circle. Turk followed on Grandpa's heels, safely held by

him on a leash among the thronging crowds. Grandpa sat at
the end of the row with Turk at his feet between him and
Ann. He gave the dog a reassuring pat. Larry came and
whispered something in Grandfather Murray's ear. At first
the old man looked doubtful but then he nodded his head.
"Aye, between us David and I might manage that, if David
holds on to the dog," he agreed.

Ann wondered what the mysterious arrangement was, then
Helen jogged her elbow. "Look just behind us! There's the
boy who played Tom," she whispered. "He must have come
up specially from London to see his film."

"And there's Douglas Campbell and Elspeth and Tom's
aunt and uncle," Ann said in surprise, naming the principal
people in the cast. "Isn't it nice they've all been able to
come?"

They exchanged nods and smiles with the folk who had all
been working on the film.

The cinema had filled with children, a thousand of them.
Soon a film was flashed on the screen but it wasn't Turk's.
It was a short 'Walt Disney' cartoon to warm up the young
audience. The two girls waited impatiently. At last the title
FLASH THE SHEEP-DOG appeared in large letters on the
screen.

"It should be *TURK* the Sheep-Dog," Ann whispered
indignantly to Helen.

"Ssh! Turk had to take the name of the dog in the book.
They have to have it the same as the story," Helen whispered
back.

Then came the picture of Tom rolling northward in the
train through the beautiful Border country. The story un-
folded till Turk himself, as Flash, appeared on the scene.
Turk, who had been lying quietly at Grandfather Murray's
feet, sat up and uttered a low growl of surprise at the dog on
the screen.

"Quiet now! Lie down!" Grandpa told him sternly in a low voice. Ann put her arms round the dog. "Ssh! It's all right, Turk. It's *you* in the picture. Don't you know yourself?"

All the same Turk kept a wary eye on the dog in the picture throughout the showing of the film and time and again he looked up at David Murray with a puzzled glance. David reassured him with a gentle stroking of his head. To David's surprise Turk greeted the actors on the screen whom he knew with a wag of his tail.

Just before the close of the picture Larry appeared quietly at Grandfather Murray's elbow and tapped him on the shoulder. "Now!" he said. Grandfather and young David rose to their feet and crept quietly from their seats, taking Turk with them on the leash. Ann started to go with them but her father put a restraining hand on her arm. "Stay where you are, Ann. You'll see why in a minute or two." The two men and the dog disappeared in the darkness of the cinema and everyone was so intent on the ending of the story that no one but Ann saw them go.

As soon as *THE END* flickered on the screen and the house-lights went up in the theatre a gentleman appeared on the stage standing by the microphone. He was a director of the Children's Film Foundation.

"Please stay where you are, children, for another minute or two and you'll be able to see on the stage the people who took part in the film."

The audience settled down again and he beckoned and Uncle and Aunt Meggetson came on the stage from the wings to loud applause and took their bow. Then came the shepherd who had been Tom's friend, followed by Douglas Campbell and Elspeth, then Tom. The applause grew even louder.

"And now I want you to give a special clap for Mr Murray,

the man who trained Flash the Sheep-Dog," the director said.

Grandfather Murray appeared on the platform and made quite a stately bow. The enthusiastic clapping was music in his ears.

"Well done, Grandpa!" Helen cried, clapping louder than anyone else, but Ann sat there tense, waiting. She sensed there was something else to come. Suddenly the old man put two fingers to his lips and gave a couple of piercing whistles which meant "Come here!" His son was standing in the aisle at the back of the stalls. Quick as lightning he unleashed Turk and like an arrow from a bow Turk streaked down the aisle and made a tremendous leap on the platform to the master he loved.

"Stand!" said old David Murray, and man and dog stood and took their bow together. The audience went mad with delight and clapped and cheered till it seemed as if the very roof would fall in with the tremendous noise.

Ann clapped her hands in joy. "He's a *real* film star. Turk's a real film star!"

For David Murray and for Turk this was their moment of glory.

Life went smoothly by at the farm for the next few weeks. It was a good season for the lambing and most of the ewes had twin lambs. Both old and young David Murray were kept busy in the field near the farm where shelters were put up for the ewes when they gave birth to their lambs. Mrs Murray was kept busy in the kitchen too, for any very small or sickly lambs had to be brought into the warmth by the fire and fed by hand from a baby's bottle. This was a job that Helen and Ann loved doing. It was a joy to see the little lambs gain in strength and begin to stagger about the kitchen on their shaky legs.

Towards the end of April the warm sun had melted the snow in the upland pastures and the sheep with their lambs were already grazing on the lower pastures near the farm. A new brood of ducklings waddled their way down to the duck-pond. "We'll soon have to be driving the sheep to the hill pastures," young David Murray said.

"Aye," Grandfather Murray agreed, but he gave a long sigh.

His son looked sharply at him. "Are you feeling all right, Father?"

"Just a bit tired, that's all," the old man said.

"It's been a hard season with the lambing. But it's past now and we'll be able to let up a bit. At least we'll no' be needing to go out so much at night to help the ewes," young David remarked.

"That's so," his father agreed.

All the same, David looked anxiously at Grandpa and so did Mrs Murray.

"You've been a bit off your food, Grandpa, and that's not like you," she said. "Could you fancy a bowl of broth right now? There's a pot simmering on the hob."

"Well, just a spoonful or two, no more. It's true I've no' felt much like my food the past few days."

"Maybe you should keep your bed the morn, Grandpa," she suggested. "I'll bring your porridge to you in bed."

"No, no, my lassie, it's good of you, but you mustn't make an invalid of me," he told her. "I don't wish to be a trouble to you."

"It would be no trouble," she told him warmly and sincerely. All the family loved the gentle old man.

"We'll see. I'll be all right after a night in my bed. I'll be up the morn to help drive the sheep up the hill."

"You stay in bed and take your rest, Father. I'll manage fine wi' the dogs," David told him.

Next morning, however, Grandfather Murray insisted on getting up to help drive the sheep to the upland pasture although his family begged him to have a lazy day. "Och! It'll do me good to go up on the hill on a grand day like this," he told them. He whistled up the dogs and they went with him and young David to drive the first flock up the side of Makeness Kipps.

"Come ahint, Turk! Come ahint!" the old man called and Turk obediently darted back and forth behind the flock and urged them upwards. The sheep were keen to go and gave little trouble, for the grass on the hill smelled fresh and green and it was spring. The lambs thrust themselves among the flock, keeping close to their mothers and darting beneath them for a quick mouthful of their warm milk, to reassure themselves over the constant drive of the dogs and for comfort. Grandfather Murray panted a little as he went up the steep hillside after them and once his hand went to his side as if he felt a sharp pain like being out of breath. When the sheep were safely herded into a grassy hollow among the hills he went to his son.

"I think I'll go back to the farm, Davie. I don't feel too good."

"I'll go back with you, Father," David said at once. He whistled for the dogs and Garry came, but Turk was still busy running round the flock. That whistle was not his master's signal.

"Can you whistle for Turk, Father? He'll only come at your bidding."

The old man whistled but gave a wince of pain. Turk came scampering down the hill immediately. All the way down the hill he kept close to his master's heel, whimpering now and again as if he guessed something was wrong. Grandfather's face was ashen and David supported him with his arm. Mrs Murray saw them coming across the farmyard and ran out to meet them.

"Oh, Grandpa, what's wrong?" she cried, putting out a helping hand too.

"I doubt but I've whistled Turk behind the sheep for the last time," he whispered, as they helped him into a chair, then telephoned for the doctor. Turk crept closer and put his head on the old man's knee and stayed looking up at him. Grandfather Murray stretched out a hand to the dog's head.

For the time that remained Turk would not be parted from David Murray but lay beside his bed watching him all the day. It was not long before the kind, gentle old man fell into his last sleep, leaving a sad family at Glenbield and a bewildered, unhappy dog.

May was a melancholy month that year at Glenbield. The house seemed empty without Grandfather's kindly presence. Turk wandered round the farm steading, a lost soul, going from room to room in the farm-house, searching the byre and outbuildings, looking for his loved master. A strange restlessness possessed him. For a while he would sit by Grandfather's empty chair, then he would stand by the door till someone let him out. Again and again he searched the farm buildings and even the pastures, then came back to the house again, looking in every room.

"I'll have to get Turk working with the sheep again," young David Murray told his wife. "If I don't he'll die of misery, looking for my father."

The next day he called Turk to heel and set out with him and Garry to the upland pasture to round up some sheep who were moving too far over the hill. Turk followed him as far as the farm gate and then turned back.

"Hi, Turk! Come here!" David called. The dog hesitated and then came part way towards him, then turned back and looked at the farm-house door. David went back and put the leash on his collar.

"Come on, lad! You've got to learn to obey me now," he said gently, a lump rising in his throat at the dog's faithfulness to his father. "Maybe he'll be all right when he gets up on the hills again with Garry," he told Mrs Murray. Turk went with him, not eagerly as he used to do when they went on the hills, but keeping to heel and ever and again looking back at the farm-house.

When they reached the wide slopes of the hills David let Turk off the leash. He crouched down as Garry did at David's feet. David pointed to the sheep scattered on the hill-side. He wanted the dogs to gather them together and bring them towards him.

"Come by, Garry!" He swung his arm in an anti-clockwise

movement and Garry sped out to the right to come well behind the sheep up the hill.

"Awa' wi' you now, Turk!" David swung his arm to the left to indicate that Turk must run up the opposite side of the field to join Garry behind the sheep. This was a pincer movement the dogs had often executed together to bring the flock towards the centre of the field. Turk started out, but not at his usual speed, stopped half-heartedly, turned and came back. This was not the voice that usually gave him commands. He looked bewildered.

"Go on, Turk!" David waved an arm in the direction the dog should take. Turk ran a short distance in the right direction, then turned round and came back to where David was standing and looked up at him with pathetic searching eyes. David shook his head sadly and fondled the dog.

"Poor Turk! You canna' understand why Grandpa's not here, can you? You miss him as much as any of us, but we'll both have to keep trying to get used to it."

Garry was bringing the flock down the hill alone, running backwards and forwards behind them.

"Good lad, Garry!" David Murray went to the gate between that field and the lower one and held it wide open. "Fetch them through the gate, Garry. You too, Turk!"

Garry knew well enough what was required of him and began to urge the sheep through the gate. David thought Turk would join Garry at driving the sheep through the gate, but Turk went behind them half-heartedly and several sheep turned and escaped him and had to be rounded up by Garry.

"This is no' you, Turk," David Murray said with a sigh. "We'll see how you do tomorrow."

The next day brought no improvement, however, nor the next, nor the next. Turk did not seem to hear any of young David Murray's commands. He went roaming round the pastures, following a scent here and there which seemed to lead him nowhere. Always, though, he came back to the farm and went round searching constantly, the kitchen, the parlour, the outhouses and the byre. He spent long hours lying outside the closed door of the room that had been Grandfather's bedroom, as if he expected the master whom he had loved so much to emerge.

"It's no good. I canna do anything with him," David told his wife. "He belonged to my father and he feels he still belongs to him. He's a one-man dog. I wonder if he might forget Father if he went somewhere else?"

"Oh, David, you wouldna' sell him, would you?"

"Sell him? No, my lass, I couldna' do that. My father thought so much of him. He said he'd never had a dog who'd been such a companion, and Turk just about worshipped him. That's the root of the trouble."

"What'll you do then?" she asked.

"Perhaps it would be a good idea to send him away for a short time. Everything here reminds him of my father. At the end of the month John Sinclair is coming to see me about some young ewes. I'll suggest that he takes Turk back with him to help at the shearing time. John did say he could do with an extra dog. Maybe a change of voice giving Turk commands will set him working the sheep again. Once he's got working again, then we can try him back here."

"You *will* have him back, Davie?" she begged.

"Oh, aye! I wouldna' part with him for good for my father's sake. The girls think a lot of him, forbye."

David Murray put his predicament to John Sinclair. "The dog spends all his time wandering round, searching, searching. He never stops looking for my father."

"I can understand that, David. Your father had a rare way with a dog—always all the patience in the world with his training and never a harsh word or a blow."

"Yes, he always said kindness with firmness was the best

teacher. You're kind to your dogs too, John. Will you take Turk over to Biggar for the sheep-shearing and see if you can get him to answer to your commands?"

"Aye, I'll do that for you, David. When he sees the other dogs working with me at the shearing, maybe he'll fall into line too. We can but try."

"Whatever happens, we'd like him back again later on, John."

"Oh, aye. That's understood."

So, in June, Turk went with John Sinclair in the back of his Landrover to Biggar. He tried to get out when he was put into the vehicle but David said sternly, "Sit!" and closed the door firmly upon him. As the Landrover climbed the steep hill Turk stood on the back seat, his paws resting on the window frame, looking back unhappily at the farm until the curve of the hill hid it from sight.

That night Turk slept in a dog basket in the farm kitchen. In the ordinary course of things John Sinclair would have given the dog a bed in the byre or the stable where he kept his other sheep-dogs but he did not want to face Turk with strange dogs till he had got used to them and they had accepted him.

"He's come here to be re-trained. He misses old David so much that he won't take commands from anyone else," he explained to Mrs Sinclair.

"He was the dog who was Flash in the film show, wasn't he?" she said, petting the dog. "He's beautiful."

"Aye, he's handsomely marked. He was doing well at the Trials too for a young dog but he's kind of gone to pieces since he lost his master. We'll make a bit of a fuss of him and maybe that will help."

Turk responded to their kindness by licking Mrs Sinclair's hand and lying down at her feet. This was a new place to him and he stared about the kitchen. He missed the girls, and most of all he missed Grandfather Murray, but in his mind he knew that David Murray was not connected with this new, strange place. There was no scent of him here. It was no use searching for him. He settled down in his basket and closed his eyes, worn out by the past month of dog-like grief.

"There! He's settling. Another week or two of different sights and smells and he'll have forgotten about Glenbield."

John Sinclair shook his head. "I doubt if dogs do forget so easily. I'll set him to work tomorrow to drive the sheep down to the farm for the shearing," the farmer decided.

Shearing is sometimes done by hand with large hand shears but more often nowadays by electrically operated clippers, something like those used by a barber but larger. The sheep cannot be sheared by the electric clippers if their coats are wet, so the day before the shearing, they are brought in from the pasture and housed in the farm buildings overnight in case of rain. It is necessary to make sure the sheep's fleeces are quite dry so that they will not suffer any electric shock.

The following day John Sinclair let Turk run with the other dogs behind the flock but he did not give him any direct commands. "We'll let that wait a while till he's got used to us," he told his farm-workers.

Turk came down with the other dogs behind the sheep, driving them to the farm, but he showed very little interest in penning them in the big empty barn. These were not *his* sheep and the farmer who gave commands to the other dogs was not *his* master. Turk felt the sheep belonged to the other dogs and it was their job to see to them being penned. He watched them for a few minutes, lifting first one forepaw and then the other, but he did not attempt to join them. As the sheep began to disappear inside the barn Turk grew bored and he went nosing round the other farm buildings.

John Sinclair missed him when the job of penning the

sheep was finished, and he went to look for him. He found
Turk just outside the farmyard gate and looking with some
interest at the woods beyond the pasture. He could smell
rabbits. Sometimes Grandfather Murray had whistled him
back from rabbiting in the woods near Glenbield. Perhaps up
there, in those woods, Turk wondered, he might find his old
master?

"Hi, Turk! Come here, Turk!" John Sinclair called to
him. Turk hesitated and then, the habit of obedience still
strong in him, he returned through the farm gate. Mr Sinclair
hooked a finger through his collar and took him back to the
farm-house.

"Take Turk inside for a while, will you?" he said to his
wife. "I just caught him wandering outside the gate. I don't
want him to run off and get lost. We must try to keep him
inside the farmyard when he's not working, until he gets
more settled."

"How's he doing?" Mrs Sinclair asked.

John Sinclair shook his head. "No' very weel, that's a fact.
He soon lost interest in the sheep after the drive down. I think
we've got a task in front of us."

He went back to the barn and Turk willingly went with
Mrs Sinclair to the farm kitchen. There was a good smell of
baking there as there was at Glenbield, but Turk did not
forget the smell of rabbits in the wood up the hill either. In
his dog-mind he decided to investigate it when the chance
offered.

Next day was a fine sunny day and the sheep-shearing
started. The sheep were penned in the farmyard. The
shearing machine with its electrically-operated clippers was
set up near the entrance. It was the task of the dogs to single
out a sheep and drive it into the pen beside the shearer. He
seized it and threw it on its back. It is difficult for a sheep to
rise from this position. Then, with lightning speed the

shearer set to work to shear the fleece, working from the stomach upwards towards the ridge of the sheep's back. Then he rolled the sheep over on the other side and sheared downwards from the backbone to the underside. When he had finished, the fleece came off all in one piece like a coat. All the time he was shearing, one of the sheep-dogs crouched nearby and set the sheep with the power of his eye; then the shearer righted the animal and said "Awa', now!" and the dog drove it out by a second gate into the farmyard. Another farm-worker seized the fleece, spread it out flat on the floor of the barn and rolled it up, thrusting any odd locks of wool in the middle. The bewildered sheared sheep hardly knew what had happened to it. It looked so much *thinner* that even a ewe's lamb looked startled at the sight of its mother.

John Sinclair let Turk watch the other dogs for a while, hoping he would take his cue from them. When the men stopped for their mid-morning drink of tea, he decided to let Turk try to single a sheep and drive it into the shearing pen. Turk had done this often at Glenbield but under Grandfather Murray's orders. When John Sinclair cried, "Come ahint, Turk!" and pointed to a sheep Turk made a half-hearted pass to get behind the sheep, then left it.

"That's no good at all, Turk!" John Sinclair shouted in exasperation. Turk knew the farmer was not pleased with him and he went slinking away with his tail between his legs. The dog longed for the kind, patient voice to which he had been accustomed. John Sinclair realised his mistake and that it was no use getting angry with the dog. He left Turk free to wander about the farmyard and watch the other dogs for a time, then he said to Jock, his shearer, "Glenbield dogs were well-known for the power of the eye. We'll see if Turk can hold the sheep with the power of his eye while it's being sheared and drive it out afterwards." He called Turk and whistled the dog to him. Turk came towards him uncertainly.

"Well, at least he's coming to me. That's one step forward," John Sinclair said.

He pointed to the sheep lying on the ground in the pen and said, "Down! Watch it!" to Turk. Turk crouched down obediently and kept his eye on the sheep.

"Now we're really getting somewhere," John Sinclair said with satisfaction.

At the words "Up!" and "Come ahint!" Turk stood up and chivvied the sheep out of the pen to rejoin those already shorn. For the next two or three sheep he obeyed the drill well, then Mrs Sinclair called John to the phone. Turk continued to set the sheep which was being sheared for a minute or two, then it was as if he realised that there was no one to tell him what to do. He took his eye off the sheep, looked about him, then rose to his feet. Immediately the warning eye was removed the sheep struggled in the shearer's hands and the clippers slipped and inflicted a slight cut on the animal. The sheep let out a pitiful bleat. Jock looked quickly at Turk. The dog had actually turned his back on the sheep and was looking for John Sinclair who had given him the command to watch it!

"Hi, you!" the shearer called angrily after Turk. It was a point of pride in a shearer to wield the clippers so skilfully that he did not inflict any cuts on the sheep. Turk stood still uncertainly. He recognised the anger in the voice and he did not know what to do. Jock did not want to relinquish his hold on the struggling sheep but he called quickly to his assistant who folded the fleeces, "Tom, get the hold of the dog and make him crouch down again."

Tom seized hold of Turk and gave him a light but slightly painful slap on the muzzle, the most tender part of a dog's body. "Down!" he cried.

Turk had never been struck in his life before. He gave a yelp of indignation as well as pain and growled at Tom. Tom lifted his hand as if to strike him again but Turk quickly backed away, turned, took a leap over the fence and was away like a streak of lightning towards the woods.

"You shouldna' have struck him, Tom," Jock said. "Mr Sinclair will be in a rare taking-on now the dog's run away and we'll be at the job of searching the woods to look for him if the dog's no' back very soon."

"Och! The dog'll find his way back soon enough when he's hungry," Tom said.

"Aye, but the dog doesna' belong to Mr Sinclair. He's just on loan from Glenbield."

Turk had made a bee-line for the woods. The wind blew a scent of rabbits towards him. He forgot the sheep, the blow on the muzzle, his own hurt feelings as he broke happily through the fence into the woods. Sometimes he had hunted rabbits near Glenbield. Perhaps here among the woods he might find the man for whom he was seeking?

When tea-time came and Turk had not returned Mr Sinclair and the two men went in search of him. Jock had told Sinclair what had happened.

"It was just a wee slap I gave him across the muzzle, no' enough to hurt him really, Mr Sinclair," Tom said. "Why, I've given my own dog many a wee slap and it doesna' upset him. I tell you, mister, I didn't really hurt the dog."

"I believe you, Tom, but I wish it hadn't happened. Well, we'd better spread out as we go through the wood and keep giving a whistle. If the dog appears, get the hold of him gently and give the others of us a shout."

They searched the wood thoroughly and came up on the hill behind it where the highway streaked across the moor but had found neither sight nor sound of Turk.

"*Now* what do we do?" Sinclair asked.

"Maybe while we've been searching for him he'll have found his way back to the farm," Jock suggested.

"We'll go back and see."

But Turk had not turned up at the farm either.

"Do you think he could have found his way across country to Glenbield?" Mrs Sinclair suggested.

"He might, at that. He's been gone a few hours now," John Sinclair agreed. "I'll have to ring up young David Murray anyway and tell him his dog's gone a-missing. He'll take it badly, I know. He set great store by his father's dog," he said heavily.

"If you let him know now, he can be on the look-out for Turk turning up at Glenbield," Mrs Sinclair said, feeling pretty sure in her own mind that the dog was on his way there and anxious to reassure her husband. Without another word John Sinclair rose unhappily from his chair and went towards the phone.

At Glenbield David Murray listened to Sinclair's unfortunate story. "No, he's not come back here," he replied. "But it's a fair distance and he may still be on his way. Meanwhile, will you notify the police at Biggar and the farms round about you, please, John? I don't want some farmer taking a pot-shot at the dog if Turk's got among his sheep and is maybe taken for a sheep worrier."

"I'll do that," Sinclair promised. "And—and I'm right sorry, David. I'll do all I can to get the dog back."

"I know you will, John."

David turned away from the phone to break the news to his family. "Turk's gone a-missing. Sinclair can't find him. It—it only wanted that——" David's voice broke on a note of sorrow.

Turk pushed his way among the undergrowth in the wood, sniffing here and there, hunting the elusive scent of rabbit. Every now and again he would lift his nose from the ground and stand with his ears erect, listening. He was listening for a whistle but it was not the whistle of John Sinclair nor any man in the valley below the wood. It was for the whistle of old David Murray, the man he had loved.

The rabbits were wary. In their burrow they caught the scent of the dog and they stayed there; besides, it was early afternoon when most rabbits dozed in their underground homes. It was not till the evening that they would come out to play on the hill-side and to look for food. Turk knew it was the wrong time to be hunting and after a while he gave up nosing out their scent. He came out of the woods on the far side from John Sinclair's farm and he looked uncertainly about him. Beyond the wood was a stretch of moorland over which there wound the white-ribbon of a high-road which crossed a silver tinkling river. Turk suddenly felt thirsty. He plunged downhill to the river and eagerly lapped water from a shallow pool. He even made darting motions with one fore-paw at the minnows swimming in it but they were too quick for him and disappeared like small silver streaks. Soon he got tired of the sport and bounded up the bank from the river again. He went up among the bracken of the moorland.

Turk did not know that most of the time he had been under observation. Two men lay concealed among the bracken on a little hillock.

"See that dog?" one of them said, as Turk emerged from the woodland. "Where's he come from?"

"He looks like a sheep-dog. There's a farm down there in the valley. I saw them rounding up the sheep yesterday for the shearing."

"Then what's the dog doing away from the sheep?"

"Poaching rabbits, likely."

"Looks like he's kind of lost to me. He looks a good dog. Say, Mike, we could use a dog like that."

"Not round here, Bill," Mike said cautiously. "They'll be out whistling him home soon and he might make back to the farm."

"We could soon have him well away from here. The van's standing in that quarry just alongside the road. It should be easy to get him into it. This isn't the only sheep farm. What d'you say we take the van along and find another farm with sheep still on the hills and lie low till tonight?"

"It's an idea, Bill," Mike agreed. "But first we'll have to entice the dog to us. Have you got a rabbit or fish you can spare in that sack?"

"Aye, there's a small rabbit, but I'm not wasting the salmon on a stray dog," Bill said.

They had already been doing some poaching along a lonely stretch of the river bank and had caught a twelve-pound salmon and some trout before they had hidden their van in the quarry and concealed themselves and the sack under the bracken in the cleft of the hill. They were waiting for night to fall to continue their operations, poaching rabbits and salmon, sheep-stealing, anything that came their way. It was safer to hide and to take a nap on the moorland than in the van.

"We'll need a bit of rope to fasten on to the dog's collar too."

"Here's a piece," Bill said, diving into the sack. " I always keep a piece handy for trussing up a sheep."

"Right! I'll whistle the dog up." Mike put his two fingers to his mouth and gave a couple of quick whistles like a shepherd, whistles that meant "Come here!"

Turk was alerted at once. He looked sharply in the direction of the whistle, got the men's scent, and then spotted them standing on the hillock. He moved uncertainly towards them.

"Come on, lad!" Mike said in a false, caressing voice, and he made a hissing noise between his teeth which always attracts a dog. Turk approached nearer. Bill brought out the rabbit and held it out towards Turk. The rabbit smelled good to Turk. He was feeling hungry. Sheep-dogs are only fed once a day, in the evening, and it seemed a long time since the meal the previous day. He was lured by the rabbit and the men seemed friendly. He trotted up to them. Bill let him sniff the rabbit though he still held on to it while he patted the dog.

"Quick with that rope, Mike," he said. Just as Turk was about to sink his teeth into the rabbit Mike smartly slipped the rope through Turk's collar. "Got him!" he cried.

Bill withdrew the rabbit and thrust it back into the sack. Turk was astonished. He leaped up at the sack but the rope through his collar restrained him.

"Come on, you!" Mike said roughly and gave the rope a jerk. Surprised, Turk resisted, splaying out his four feet on the ground, but Mike pulled harder and dragged the dog after him.

Bill went in front and dangled the sack containing the rabbit just before Turk's nose. "Wait a minute, Mike," he said. "You know the old saying, 'Let the dog see the rabbit'?" He pulled the rabbit out of the sack and held it just beyond Turk's reach. The rope went slack as Turk followed the new lure. They reached the van hidden in the worked-out roadside quarry. Bill had the doors open in a trice and he jumped into the van, holding out the rabbit to Turk who leaped in after him. Mike followed.

"Get that spare sack, Mike, and shove it over the dog's head," Bill said. Once more he withdrew the rabbit. Turk barked indignantly at being cheated. Mike released the rope and Turk's barks were suddenly muffled as the sack descended over his head. Mike quickly tied the mouth of the sack with the rope.

"You lie there and be quiet!" he shouted at Turk. He gave a cruel kick at the sack which caught Turk in the ribs and made him yelp with pain.

"Hi! Don't damage the dog, Mike, or he'll be no use to us. Besides, who knows? There may be a reward out for him in a few days. We'd better get away out of here and thirty miles or so south with him. It's good sheep country down by Moffat and there's a number of roads we can use for a get-away from there. We could cut back to Glasgow and get rid of any sheep we get tonight to a butcher I know."

"All right. It's not a bad scheme. I hope no one hears that brute yelping away in the back of the van though."

"He'll not be heard above the noise of the engine," Bill assured Mike. "Besides, we'll be moving too fast for anyone to take much notice of a noise coming from the van."

"Let's get moving then."

The van sped away south towards Moffat but Bill did not drive right into the town. That might be asking for trouble if a curious policeman heard the dog and looked into the van. He turned up a steep road among the moors. Here he stopped the van and drew to the side of the road behind a screen of trees.

"I reckon there'll not be many cars along this road. We can have a kip here till it's dark, then we'll drive back to the road again. There are sheep on the hill-side down yonder. It shouldn't take us long to round up two or three. The dog'll help to gather them and drive them to the van. Then we'll get back through Moffat at first light."

"And what if we're stopped going through Moffat?" Mike was always full of gloomy forebodings.

"We'll say we're on our way to the sheep sales at Lanark. You want to use your loaf, man! Who's likely to think there's anything amiss when we've got our sheep-dog with us?" Bill winked. He was always the one to take a chance.

In the van Turk growled but he did not bark. He was exhausted with barking earlier and was half-suffocated in the sack. "I'll settle him!" Mike threatened.

"Leave him be!" Bill advised. "Just get a nap yourself for we'll have to be on the move as soon as it's dark enough."

The men settled themselves into the cab of the van and fell into an uneasy sleep. Turk also closed his eyes. There was nothing else he could do but lie still and wait till the sack was taken away.

Twilight was fading into night when Mike stirred. He

shook Bill by the shoulder. "Come on! Time to get going."
Bill was awake in an instant, yawned, shook himself, started
the engine and let in the clutch. Turk awakened too and
gave a sharp bark as the van jolted forward. In another
minute they were careering down the mountain road to its
juncture with the road leading to Moffat. Up on the right
the ground climbed to the high moors dotted with sheep. It
was the time of the year when the sheep stayed out on the
hills all night.

Bill pulled up where the road made a wide curve. "This
should be a good place. Not too far to get the sheep into the
van. Half a dozen should be enough. We'll not be greedy,"
he grinned. "Let's get the dog on the rope and give him a
scamper along the road first. If he's like me, he'll be feeling
a bit stiff."

Turk came backward out of the sack and as soon as his
head emerged Mike slipped the rope through his collar.
Turk looked dazed at first but when he saw the van door
open, he made a leap to get out. The rope brought him up
short.

"Oh no, you don't!" Mike said. "You come along with
me."

He jerked the dog down on to the road beside him and
began a jog-trot along the road. This Turk understood and
he ran alongside the man, glad to be on the road again. After
a few hundred yards Mike returned to the van. "Ready
now?" he said to Bill. "That should have limbered him up."

Bill was eating a hunk of bread and cold bacon. He held
out a crust to Turk with a bit of the bacon on it. Turk devoured it hungrily. "Dog's hungry!" Bill said.

"Aye, well, we'll keep him that way till he's done his job
with the sheep," Mike replied.

"He's got a brass plate on his collar. What's the name on
it?" Bill said idly, examining it by the light of the van lamps.

"It says *Turk, Glenbield*. Glenbield? Maybe a farm somewhere near Biggar?"

"Take the collar off him. The police may have been told to look out for him. We can put it on him again once we've got rid of the sheep and watch out for any reward for him. He looks a valuable dog," Mike said.

"We'll need the collar to slip the rope through," Bill said.

"Och, then, we'll take off the brass plate. It should come off easy enough with a knife. Slip the rope round his neck while I take the collar off."

Mike worked away with a sharp knife at the brass tab and soon had it off. He slipped it in his pocket. "We can fix it on again if we put in for a reward," he said, putting the collar round Turk's neck again.

"At least we know the dog's name. Perhaps he'll answer to it?" Bill suggested. "Turk! Come on, Turk!"

Turk gave an answering "Wuff!" when he heard his name.

"Right! Come on. Let's go," said Mike.

With Turk still on the rope they climbed up the bank at the side of the road and into the rough moorland pasture stretching up the hill. In the midsummer half-dark they could just distinguish the ghost-like forms of sheep towards the summit. Cautiously and quietly the two men climbed the hill. Turk had been trained not to bark at sheep and he was quiet too. Some of the sheep were lying down, some munching at the short, sweet grass. Stealthy though the men were, the sheep scented the dog and those lying down rose to their feet. The sheep began to huddle together in a flock for their greater protection and to move away from the advancing group. Mike took the rope from Turk's neck. "Come ahint, Turk!" he cried, moving his arm to the right.

Turk knew well enough he had to run out in a wide circling arc behind the flock. He sped to the right and came down the hill behind the flock which began to hustle towards the two men.

"He's a good dog," Bill said. "Maybe we'll keep him."

"Wait till he's finished the job," Mike muttered, then he shouted, "Stop, Turk! Stop!"

Still Turk drove the flock before him. The sheep began to run.

"Doesn't the brute understand? He'll have the flock stampeding."

"Try whistling!" Bill suggested. "He'll be more used to whistle signals. I think one long blast means 'Stop!'"

Mike put his fingers to his mouth and whistled. Turk slowed down but he did not stop altogether. This was not the whistle he knew. The flock slowed down to a walking pace.

"Give him two short whistles now. I think shepherds do that to tell their dogs to come on," Bill said.

Mike whistled again and once more Turk began to move the flock. They began to run. Mike waved his arms wildly to indicate to Turk that he wanted the dog to bring some sheep to him but not the whole flock. Turk could not understand these wild signals and he darted at the sheep once more, thinking he had to divide the flock. The flock scattered in a panic to right and left, some heading up the hill again, bleating noisily.

"Drat the dog! The sheep are making enough noise to wake the dead. In a few minutes we'll have the farmer coming to see what's up." Mike swore at Turk, threatening him with a stick.

"I've got hold of one sheep here. Give me a hand to carry it to the van," Bill said.

By the time they had the sheep into the van the rest of the flock was away up to the summit of the hill again with Turk behind them.

"Stop the dog or he'll drive them down over the other side to the farm," Bill exclaimed.

Mike gave his long, piercing whistle. This time Turk stopped.

"Come here! Come here!" Mike shouted.

Turk hesitated, bewildered by the contradictory commands. Once more he started driving the sheep downhill, expecting a steadying whistle but it did not come. The sheep plunged downhill towards the trees.

"Hang the dog! He'll have them on the road and any cars coming by will have to stop. We'll be for it then!" Bill exclaimed. "Drive the sheep back up the hill and get hold of the dog."

Waving their arms frantically the men rushed in front of the oncoming flock. The sheep hesitated, panicked and scattered, baaing louder than ever. Turk came round the flock towards the men, thinking he must drive the sheep up the hill again. He was stopped only a few yards away by Mike's prolonged whistle. He crouched on the ground between the men and the flock. Mike rushed up to him and grabbed his collar while Bill ran towards the sheep, sending them stampeding again.

Mike lashed savagely with his piece of rope at Turk as he held him by the collar. Turk yelped piteously. He had never been thrashed before. He did not know what he had done wrong. Now he had driven the sheep down to the men as the whistle seemed to command and they had driven the sheep back again. This was an unjust beating and all dogs deeply resent injustice. Turk squirmed, his one intent to get away from the cruel lash. Bill came running back. "Steady on, Mike!" he cried. "We'll get no reward for the dog if you've marked him."

Just then Turk turned and snapped at Mike's hand holding his collar. He had never snapped at anyone before but pain drove him to it. His teeth scarred Mike's hand. Mike let go the collar and aimed a savage kick at Turk which sent

him rolling headlong down the steep bank above the road, unable to stop himself. At that moment a large car came round the bend of the road and the bumper struck Turk on the head and leg. The force of the blow sent Turk sprawling unconscious on the road.

"I think we hit something just now," the driver said to his

passenger. "I hope it wasn't a sheep. I'm not stopping to find out. I've no time if we're to get the train at Carlisle."

The car speeded on and Turk lay quite still in the road.

Mike and Bill waited till the sound of the car died away in the distance, then they went down to the road and looked at Turk. Bill bent over the dog and touched him with his foot. Turk did not stir. "He's done for," Bill said.

"He wasn't much use to us anyway," Mike said angrily.

"No, but we can't claim any reward for a dead dog," Bill reminded him. "You shouldn't have let your temper get the better of you, Mike. He might have been good for a reward of a fiver."

"We'd better get out of here as quick as we can," Mike decided. "Remember we've still got that sheep in the van and some poached salmon too."

"Where's the brass plate off the dog's collar?" Bill asked.

"Here in my pocket."

"Then we'd better chuck it away and the collar off the dog too. If we're unlucky and we're stopped by the police they might search us. We don't want to be connected with a dead dog and a sheep missing from a flock." He stooped and quickly unstrapped the collar from Turk's neck. The dog did not stir. "Here, give me the brass plate," Bill said to Mike. He ran down to the river on the other side of the road and threw the collar and brass plate well out into the deepest current. "Now there's nothing to connect us with the dead dog," he said. "Let's get the van started and out of here before anything else comes along the road. We were lucky that chap didn't stop. We'll just leave the dog where he is."

Bill started the van and drove down the rutted track behind the trees back to the road again, then he drove off quickly in the direction of the main road to Glasgow. Turk still lay motionless on the road.

The furniture removal van swerved to the right and the driver braked. "What's that lying in the road?" he asked his mate.

"Looks like a dead dog to me."

The driver jumped down to the road and bent over Turk. Just then Turk's ears twitched slightly. The driver put out a hand and touched him. "He's still warm and breathing," he told his mate. "It looks as if he's been hit by a car. His head's bleeding." He touched the dog gently. Turk's eyes opened. He raised his head and whined a little. The driver patted him gently on his shoulder. "He's coming round. Looks like he's

been knocked unconscious." He spoke soothingly to Turk. "It's all right, old chap. Come on, now."

Turk wagged his tail feebly at the sound of the kindly sympathetic voice.

"He looks like a sheep-dog to me," the driver's mate said. "Maybe he's from a farm nearby."

"Farmers don't usually let their sheep-dogs stray along the road," the truck driver replied. "He's not wearing a collar, so there's no telling where he's come from. Strange, that, for there look to be the marks of a collar on his neck. Perhaps he'll make his own way home now he's come round." He spoke encouragingly to Turk. "Come on, lad! Get on your feet again. Up, now!"

Turk understood the word "Up!" and struggled to rise but his foreleg gave way under him and he collapsed on the road again.

"His leg's broken, poor beast!" the driver exclaimed.

"What'll we do with him then, Tom?" the mate asked.

For a minute or two Tom looked perplexed. "We can't leave him lying here. Another car or truck might come along and put finished to him."

"Shall we lift him up onto the bank then?"

"The poor beast needs attention. He might die if he's left on the bank, Jack. He's got more injuries than just that leg, I think. There's a gash over his ribs. We'd better get him onto the van."

"We can't go round the farms hereabouts to see if they've lost a dog," Jack told him. "Besides, we're due in Wigan with this load of furniture by the morning."

"Aye, Jack, you're right there, but this poor animal needs attention from a vet. He's a bonnie dog and I don't like to think of him lying in pain." Tom patted Turk gently again and Turk gave a grateful lick to his hand. That decided Tom. "We'll take him with us, Jack and find a vet somewhere, maybe in Wigan. It'll be morning by the time we get there. Get that bit of sacking out from the van. We can make him comfortable between us. Then help me lift him. I don't want to haul him about too much."

Jack arranged the sacking on the seat, then he and Tom together lifted Turk on to it. Turk felt the voices and hands were gentle and kind and he did not resist though he whined at the pain of being moved. Tom stroked his head gently, avoiding the wound, and Turk licked his hand and relaxed. Tom turned his attention to driving again. After a while the movement of the van sent Turk to sleep. Tom drove steadily on till they pulled in at a night-café for long-distance drivers.

"Fetch me a mug of tea, Jack. I'll stay in the cab to keep an eye on the dog," Tom said. "Oh, and bring a bowl of milk for him. He's licking his tongue out as though he's thirsty."

When the milk was set beside Turk he lapped it up, hardly pausing. He gave a lick to his injured leg and then settled down to sleep again. Once more the van rolled through the night, up and down the long road over Shap Fell, over bridges across rivers, through the sleeping streets of towns. Turk stirred now and again to change his position slightly and to huddle closer to Tom. Each mile took him further from his native Scotland but Turk was not aware of that. He was content to lie beside his new friend and to feel the warmth of him. All the same, he lifted his head from time to time and sniffed the air, registering the strange scents in his memory.

The furniture van travelled steadily down the A6 road till dawn. After Preston it took the A49 that branched to Wigan. The towns crowded close together in the industrial belt of south Lancashire. Great cotton mills reared their many-windowed walls skywards; the twin wheels of colliery winding gear stood high above the brick houses ranged in long rows of narrow streets; murky silent canals threaded their way across the land. Here and there was a flash of green parkland and a waving field of green corn ripening for harvest but the fields and farms grew fewer as the van headed south. Lancashire was a great sprawl of mining and manufactures and the hum of industry filled the air.

Turk raised his head and looked about him. He knew houses and streets, for David Murray had often taken him to the Friday market in Peebles, but they were not houses like these red brick ones, neither were there towering factories. He sniffed the air and many strange unknown scents came to him but the familiar scent of sheep was not among them. He dropped his head, puzzled. This was a new world of unfamiliar scents.

The shop assistants were hurrying to their work as the van rumbled through the old Market Place of Wigan, past the waiting buses. Behind a huge store the clock in the old Parish Church chimed a quarter to nine.

"We've made pretty good time, Tom," Jack remarked.

"Not bad," Tom agreed.

"Will you go straight to the house or have the dog looked to first?"

Tom considered. "I think we'd better go and see the chap at the house first. He'll be waiting on this furniture coming. I'm not quite sure where to take the dog. I could go to the police but that would take up time and I'd like the dog seen to right away. Maybe the chap we're taking this load to has a phone book that would give a vet's name. The boss told me he's a doctor who's lived here a while. This is his mother-in-law's furniture we've got. She's going to live with him."

Tom turned south to the outskirts of Wigan. The road climbed steadily uphill. Nearly three miles out of the city, on the top of another hill, Tom drew up outside a double-fronted red-brick house bright with white paint and cheerful gay curtains.

"This'll be the place. It says 'Orrell Knoll' on the gate."

Tom scrutinised a brass plate fixed to the gate. "Dr Jarvis," he read. "Aye, this is it." He opened the gate wide.

The front door of the house was flung open and a boy and a girl rushed out shouting to someone inside the house, "Dad! Dad! Grandma's furniture's come."

A tall man with sandy hair turning grey at the temples, followed them through the door.

"Ah, you're from Locke's, bringing the furniture? Good! You'd better run the van up the drive to the front door so you can unload there."

Tom steered the van carefully up the gravel drive. As he jumped down from the driver's cab Turk tried to rise to his feet to follow him but Tom said firmly, "No! Lie down!" Turk understood that command and did as he was told.

"Will you show us where you want us to put the furniture, sir?" Tom asked.

"We've got a couple of rooms ready." The doctor peered inside the cab of the van. "You've got your dog with you, I see."

"He's not mine. We found him lying injured on a road in Scotland. I think he must have been knocked down by a car. He's got a broken leg and a head injury and maybe a cracked rib too. I'm going to take him to a vet as soon as we've unloaded the furniture. Perhaps you could recommend one, sir?"

"I'll take a look at him first. The furniture can wait a few minutes. Carry him into the kitchen. This way."

Tom gently cradled Turk in his arms and carried him in. He was followed by the two children who eyed the dog with pity.

"Put him on the kitchen table," Dr Jarvis said.

Turk gave a little whine as the doctor examined his leg but he seemed to know the gentle hands were trying to help him.

"Yes, the leg's broken and will have to be set. He seems to have a couple of cracked ribs too and there's a big swelling on his head where the blood has dried over a cut."

"He'd been knocked unconscious when we found him. We thought he was dead at first," Tom explained.

"I *could* set the leg but I think it's really a job for a vet. He'll have the right instruments and anaesthetic and bandages. There's a good vet just along the road."

"I'll take him there then," Tom said.

The doctor shook his head. "No. It would be better to get the vet to come here. Too much moving about will cause the dog pain and won't do his injuries any good. I'll phone Mr Muir. Just keep the dog quiet."

"Poor dog! Can I pat him?" the little girl asked.

"Very gently, then. Just here on his shoulder." Tom indicated the spot. She patted him lightly, saying "Poor, poor dog!" Turk lifted his head and gave a quick lick to her hand. He knew there was compassion in her voice. "What's his name?" she asked Tom.

"That's what I can't tell you, lassie. I just found him lying on the road and he had no collar."

The doctor came back from the phone. "Mr Muir is on his way," he announced.

"I think the dog's thirsty," the boy remarked. "He keeps licking his tongue in and out. Can I get him a bowl of water?"

"Just bring it in a saucer, Peter, and put it by his head so he can reach it without standing up."

Turk raised his head and lapped gratefully at the water. As he finished it Mr Muir arrived. After he'd examined Turk he said, "It looks as if he has had more than one blow. I would think those broken ribs were the result of a kick. Someone must have cruelly mishandled him."

"Oh, who could be so wicked?" the little girl cried.

The vet removed his jacket. "I'll just give him a painkilling injection and then I'll get to work on that leg," he decided.

"Out of the kitchen, children! Mr Muir needs plenty of room. Run along now, Susan," Dr Jarvis ordered when they were inclined to linger. "You can come back when Mr Muir has finished."

Turk was soon fast asleep after the injection and Mr Muir re-set and splinted and strapped the leg skilfully, put some elastoplast over the cracked ribs and another plaster over the gash in Turk's head. "He'll do now," he said. "Who does he belong to? I'd like to see him again in about a week."

Tom had been standing quietly by the door. He explained the circumstances under which he had found Turk. "He's not really mine but I'll pay your fee, sir."

"We'll forget the fee." Mr Muir waved it aside. "What will you do with the dog?"

"I don't know who owns him. Maybe I should hand him over to the police." Tom hesitated.

"But Mr Muir said he wanted to see the dog in a week," Susan said. "Couldn't he stay here for a bit, just till his leg's better?"

"Oh dear! I could see that coming." Dr Jarvis gave a wry smile. "All the battered beasts and birds in the neighbourhood seem to find their way here. We've had a stray tortoise that ate up all the lettuce in the garden and a pigeon with a damaged wing, to say nothing of a white mouse that got inside the settee."

"But the dog won't eat the lettuce," Susan said.

"And he certainly couldn't get inside the settee," Peter pointed out.

"He'll probably shed dog-hairs all over it instead and then what will your mother say?" the doctor asked.

Just then the door opened and Mrs Jarvis came in. She was a plump, good-natured woman with a sunny smile. She had been visiting a sick neighbour. "What will I say to what?" she asked gaily, then saw Turk lying on the table. "Good gracious!"

Everyone tried to explain to her at once. At last she got the story sorted out. "Well, the dog's not fit to go back to Scotland and we can hardly turn him out into the street," she said.

"Oh, Mother, does that mean we can keep him?" Susan clapped her hands eagerly.

Mrs Jarvis hesitated for a minute. "All right, we'll keep him just till he's better but if he turns out to be surly or snappy or dirty in the house, you must understand, Susan, he'll have to go."

"I think he's quite a good-tempered dog, ma'am," Tom said.

"What's his name?"

"That I don't know. He'd got no collar. He's a sheep-dog, Border collie, you know, probably belonging to a sheep farmer who'll be in a right taking-on at losing him. When I go to that district again I'll make enquiries, but I'm not often there. I'd have gladly had him myself but I live in lodgings and I'm away a lot driving the van." Tom sounded regretful.

"If he hasn't got a name, then can we give him one?" Susan asked. "Then he'll come when we call him."

"I can see he's going to be established as a member of the family," Mrs Jarvis declared with an air of resignation. "Well, what are you going to call him?"

"There was a film at the cinema last Saturday called *Flash the Sheep-Dog*. This dog's very like Flash," Peter said, little knowing how near the truth he was.

"Yes, he *is* like Flash. Let's call him that," Susan suggested. For once the twins were in agreement.

"He'll not be much like Flash with a lame leg," Dr Jarvis remarked.

"Oh, he'll get over that all right. The dog's got stamina. He comes of a good breed," Mr Muir told them. "Well, I'd better get away on my rounds. The dog will probably sleep a lot today. Keep him quiet for a few days. When he starts walking about he'll probably go on three legs. The splint will keep the broken leg stiff. Don't encourage him to run."

"I hope he won't have to sleep on my kitchen table all day or there'll be no dinner for anyone," Mrs Jarvis laughed. "He'd be more comfortable on a hearthrug by the fire."

"I'll lift him there, ma'am," Tom offered at once. He put the sleeping dog down gently on the rug. Susan knelt beside him.

"Flash! Flash!" she whispered in his ear as she stroked his shoulder. Turk stirred a little, opened his eyes and gave a thump of his tail. Flash was a name he remembered. Once there had been a boy who had called him that and men who had made much of him when his old master had whistled him across the hill-side after the sheep. These things stirred drowsily in his memory.

"Flash! Flash!" Susan repeated. Turk gave another sleepy thump of his tail.

"He likes his name. He's answering to it already," Susan cried with delight. "I think he's a real clever dog."

"Very likely." Mrs Jarvis smiled indulgently. "Leave him alone now, Susan, and let him sleep. I hope to goodness that you children never find a stray elephant in need of care and affection, though!"

Turk drifted off into slumber again, content and warm. Tom began the job of unloading the furniture. Jack had already made a start with smaller items. Dr Jarvis looked at his watch.

"Mercy me! I'll be late for my surgery. Can you superintend the furniture going in, dear?"

"Just leave it to me," Mrs Jarvis said capably.

Peter went with her but Susan sat on the rug beside Turk to watch over him. A new life was beginning for Turk, though the Jarvis family did not know that the new life was linked to the old life by the name *Flash* they had given him.

Something of a new life was beginning for the Jarvis family too. Dr Jarvis had joined three other doctors in a partnership and a new clinic and consulting rooms had been built for them in the nearby small township of Lamberhead Green. Previously Dr Jarvis had his surgery and waiting-room in his own house. Now these two rooms were free. Just about this time Mrs Jarvis's mother, Mrs Mackay, who lived in Scotland, had an operation on her hip which left her rather lame. It was decided it would be a good idea for her to come and live with the Jarvis family and occupy the two rooms which were empty. That was why her furniture had been brought south. She was staying with a friend for six weeks until she felt well enough to travel south. Meanwhile Mrs Jarvis was getting the rooms ready to welcome her mother.

For two days Turk slept quietly by the fire, eating and drinking what was set before him. Now and again he would rise stiffly on three legs and move towards the door into the garden. Then Mrs Jarvis would let him out for a brief spell but he soon came limping back again on three legs and lapsed into sleep on the rug.

"Well, I will say he has been properly house-trained. In his way he always asks to go out. He's a clean dog," Mrs Jarvis admitted, "but he'd be the better for a bath." Turk's coat was still dusty from his tumble in the muddy road.

"As soon as he begins to run around I think we must try to give him a bath in the garden," she decided.

A few days later Turk began to show an interest in the garden, to run round it on three legs, sniffing here and there as he memorised the new scents. Mr Muir called again and examined him.

"He's doing well. Border collies are highly intelligent dogs. He knows that leg won't stand much weight yet so he keeps it lifted from the ground. When he begins to put it down again, you'll know it's well on the way to being healed."

"Can we take him for a walk yet?" Susan asked.

Mr Muir smiled. "I wouldn't advise it just yet, Susan. Be patient for a while and let him just limp round the garden at his own pace."

"Besides, we haven't taken out a licence for him yet and he needs a collar with his name on too before you start taking him for walks," Dr Jarvis pointed out.

"What about giving him a bath?" Mrs Jarvis asked practically. "I'm sure he'd be the better for it and I'd be a happier woman for I don't like a dusty dog round my kitchen."

"You'd have to be very careful," Mr Muir said. "He mustn't get that injured leg wet."

"What about turning the garden hose on him?" Peter asked practically. "That way we could spray him gently *and* keep his plastered leg dry."

Mr Muir laughed. "That might be all right, but you *must* do it gently and very carefully. Don't forget the full force of it might knock him over when he's on three legs. As soon as he starts running about naturally on four legs you can bring him for his first walk to my surgery so I can remove the plaster bandage."

The Jarvis family began to discuss how they would give Turk, Flash to them, his bath. "He'd do with a good soaping over first," Mrs Jarvis said.

"What about mixing a bowl of warm water with Lux suds?" Susan suggested.

"Lux so his coat doesn't shrink?" Peter giggled.

"Don't be daft! Will you lend me your old car sponge, Daddy?" Susan asked. "I could soap him over with that."

"If Susan soaps him then I'll *unsoap* him with the hose," Peter decided.

"Yes, but be gentle with the hose. A fine spray and not too much force behind it. Remember what Mr Muir said," Dr Jarvis reminded him.

Susan prepared her bowl of suds and called Turk to follow her into the garden. "Flash! Flash, come here!"

Turk recognised the command. He followed and when Susan set the bowl down on the grass, he sniffed at it. The scent reminded him of washing day at Glenbield and he welcomed it because it was familiar.

"Stand still, Flash!" Susan commanded.

This was another command Turk understood and he obeyed. Susan put an arm round his neck and began to squeeze the soapy sponge over his back and to rub him gently with it. Turk rather liked the stroking with the sponge and the nice refreshing feel of the warm water. He stood like a rock, wagging his tail with pleasure. Susan carefully avoided getting the soap in his eyes and the almost healed cut on his head. Turk loved her gentle, caressing hands. David Murray had washed him like this when he was getting him ready for the Sheep-Dog Trials. Then, after he was soaped David would take him for a plunge in the river to get rid of the soap suds. Turk began to look about the garden wondering where the river was.

"Stand still, Flash!" Peter cried. Once more Turk obeyed,

then he got a horrid shock. A drenching heavy spray seemed to descend on him from the sky. He stood there for a moment bewildered, blinded by the spray while the suds made a pool round his feet. He jumped aside.

"Stand still, Flash!" Peter bellowed again. Turk made a half-hearted attempt to obey, then rushed for cover into the kitchen. Round and round the table he ran on his three legs, stopping now and again to shake the drops from his soaking coat. In vain Mrs Jarvis tried to get hold of him to drag him outside again.

"Call him, Peter! Call the dog!" she shouted.

"Come here, Flash!" Peter called.

Turk took one look outside the door but Peter was still standing with the hose in his hand, the spray from it showering on the lawn. Turk had had enough of that strange bath! He bolted back into the kitchen again and began shaking vigorously once more.

"Oh, just look at the floor and the furniture!" Mrs Jarvis lamented.

Susan was a resourceful child. She rushed into the wash-house and seized a bath sheet from the soiled-linen basket. "Come here, Flash! Come here!" she cried.

Turk recognised her voice. He connected it with every-thing pleasant in his new experiences; food, biscuits, a kind voice, gentle, caressing hands. This time he obeyed and ran out into the garden again, cowering back from the hose.

"Shut off that hose, Peter!" Dr Jarvis ordered. "The dog's frightened of it."

Susan held out her arms. "Come here, Flash!"

In another moment Turk was inside the enveloping towel and Susan was rubbing him down gently. Panting, he stayed quietly within the shelter of her arms.

"I don't think he's ever had a bath before!" Mrs Jarvis exclaimed.

"Oh, he'll have had a bath, but not one like that!" Dr Jarvis laughed. "More likely a swim in a river."

Mrs Jarvis was looking regretfully at her once clean and shining kitchen. "I hope he doesn't do this every time he has a bath or I'll be sorry I let the children keep him."

"Oh, once his leg is healed Susan and Peter can hold him in the old zinc bath we keep in the greenhouse. It won't matter if he wallops round in that if it's on the lawn."

"I shall be careful in future to keep the kitchen door closed when he has a bath. I wonder how he'll get on with Mother's poodle when she arrives with it?" she remarked apprehensively.

"We'll cross that bridge when we come to it," Dr Jarvis reassured her. "There's almost a month yet. Flash will have had time to settle down and no doubt your mother will keep the poodle in her rooms."

Mrs Jarvis looked as if she were not so sure of that.

Out on the lawn Susan was brushing and combing Turk's coat and gently getting the tangles out of it. Turk enjoyed the grooming. He remembered how Ann had brushed his coat till it shone when she got him ready for the Sheep-Dog Trials.

Before the month was up Turk was ceasing to limp and was beginning to use the damaged leg. The time came when Dr Jarvis came home from town with a collar and a leash.

"You can take Flash for his first walk as far as Mr Muir's surgery," he told the children. "I haven't got his name and address on the collar yet. A brass tab is being engraved for it but I hadn't time to wait for it today. I'll get it next week."

Susan fitted on the collar and Peter attached the leash. Turk had been used to wearing both a collar and a leash on occasions so he made no objection; he merely stretched his neck about a bit to make sure that Susan did not buckle it on too tightly. Peter gave a slight tug to the leash. "Come on, Flash! Let's go for a walk."

Turk knew that the hitching on of the leash meant a walk and he barked in happy excitement. Peter led him out of the back garden, through the side gate and down the gravel drive to the road. Just as they emerged on to the pavement a large red bus flashed by. Turk cowered back and tried to return to the garden again. The memory of the car coming at him returned. That was when he had been hurt.

"Come on, cowardy! It's only a bus," Peter told him. They took a few paces along the pavement. Traffic roared past them along the road and again Turk shrank back.

"He's frightened of the motors," Susan said, feeling very sorry for the dog. "Perhaps it's because he was injured by one."

"He can't have been used to traffic wherever he came from," Peter remarked.

They progressed a few yards further, Turk shrinking against the garden walls whenever a vehicle hurtled by. Peter began to be exasperated. "Whatever's the use of a dog if you can't take him for a walk?" he said, giving an impatient tug to the leash. "Come to heel, Flash!" he called, remembering the commands that had been given to the sheep-dog in the film he and Susan had seen. Surprisingly Turk did come to heel and with Susan's reassuring hand on his collar they got as far as the pavement opposite Mr Muir's surgery.

"Now we've got to cross the road. I hope Flash doesn't pull back," Peter said anxiously. "We don't want to hold back the traffic while we drag him across."

They had barely got a yard from the kerb when a loud siren announced the coming of a fire-engine. Turk leaped back on to the pavement dragging Peter with him. He shook with fear, his ears laid back against his head, his tail drooping. The memory of being struck by the car was still fresh. The bustle and clamour of the streets and the smell of petrol and diesel oil fumes distressed him. He looked about for the green pastures and the heather-clad moors rising to the sky and they were not there. This was strange alien country with its rows of brick houses and shops. Where were the grazing sheep that he used to round up? He could not even *smell* sheep anywhere. A wave of homesickness for the hills of the north possessed him. He was roused from it by an impatient tug on the leash.

"Will we ever get him over the road?" Peter asked crossly.

"Wait till the lights change at the cross-roads and there's a gap in the traffic. Then I'll go first and call him after me," Susan suggested.

Turk was more ready to follow Susan's call than to obey Peter's impatient tugging. There stirred in him a memory of the girls at the farm of Glenbield. Ann had loved to brush his coat as Susan did. Susan was like the girl in his memory and though he knew she was not that girl, it made it easier for him to obey her. This time they crossed the road without Turk hanging back though he showed the whites of his eyes when the buses began to roar past as the traffic lights changed.

Mr Muir looked him over carefully and removed the plaster from his leg. He looked pleased. "A good mend," he announced. "The scar on his head has healed well too and I don't think his ribs are giving him much trouble. You can let him run about freely now."

"He seems frightened of the traffic," Peter told him.

"So would you be if you were a country boy. This dog's a country lad, born and bred, I'm pretty certain. You must let him get used to the traffic gradually. Try to take him walks where there are fields and you can let him loose."

"We've got to go along a lot of busy roads before we get to fields. I don't always want to have to *drag* him along." Peter sounded impatient.

"Perhaps your father will run you out in his car to some

country spot? I know he's a busy doctor but maybe when it's his 'day off', he'll make time. This kind of dog needs lots of exercise over open hills."

"We'll tell him what you say," Peter agreed, but he sounded doubtful.

With some stops and starts they got Turk home again. Turk bounded about happily in the garden, glad to be free of the leash and the terrifying traffic.

Susan told her father what Mr Muir had said.

"Certainly I'll try to give Flash a run in the country now and again," he said. "But I can't manage it this week. I have to meet your Grandma Mackay at the station and bring her to her new home. And the week afterwards I may have to attend a medical conference in Manchester, but we'll see what can be done after that. I don't want Flash to get fat for lack of exercise."

On Saturday Grandma Mackay arrived with such a quantity of luggage and boxes that both the inside of the car and the boot were piled high. Nestling close to her in the car was a small black poodle. The children rushed to the door to meet her for they were fond of their grandmother. As Mrs Mackay hugged and kissed the children she let go the leash she had put on Nero the poodle. There was a sudden scuffle in the entrance hall. Nero had flown at Turk, snapping and leaping round him. Turk stood his ground, barking angrily at the intruder. He felt it was his job to guard the home. The two dogs spun round and round, Nero snapping and showing his teeth and Turk snarling, though he did not attempt to bite the smaller dog.

Lame as she was Mrs Mackay rushed to snatch up her pet while Peter grabbed Turk by the collar. From Mrs Mackay's arms Nero still yapped impudently at Turk but Turk's snarling subsided to a rumbling growl.

"You didn't tell me you had a dog," Mrs Mackay said in

an injured voice. "You might have warned me and I would never have set Nero down. That brute might have killed him."

"Oh, Grandma, Flash is not a brute! He's a very gentle dog really." Susan was almost in tears. "Nero flew at him first."

"Nero is not aggressive," Mrs Mackay declared indignantly.

"Flash didn't hurt him at all. If Flash had really gone for Nero he could have torn him in little pieces," Peter retorted. The welcome seemed likely to turn into an angry argument just when Dr Jarvis came in carrying a suitcase. In a moment he took in the situation.

"Take Flash out to the garden, Susan, and shut the kitchen door. I can't have scuffles going on between dogs while I'm bringing in the luggage."

"But it's Flash's home—" Peter was beginning when Dr Jarvis said firmly, "That's enough! Just give me a hand to carry the luggage to your grandma's rooms."

Susan, with tears in her eyes, led Turk to the back garden

and shut the door upon him while Mrs Jarvis said, "Come along, Mother, and I'll show you how we've arranged the furniture in your rooms. You can see if it's to your liking while I bring in the tea. Then perhaps you'd like to have a little rest after your journey."

The tea acted like oil on troubled waters but every now and again Susan went to the window to look at Turk crouching on the grass close to the back door and watching it anxiously to know when he would be re-admitted. Somehow he knew he was in disgrace and he did not know why. He had a sense of injustice that he had been wrongly reproved and turned out from the presence of the family. It was all connected somehow with the strange little black dog.

After tea Mrs Mackay said, "I'd like to give Nero a run in the garden since he's been cooped up all day in the train, but what about *your* dog? He's in the garden, isn't he? Is he likely to go for Nero again?"

Peter was about to say something angrily but his father checked him with a look. "Just put Flash in the tool-shed, Peter, and close the door. He'll take no harm there for a while."

Rather sullenly Peter obeyed and Mrs Jarvis took a deep breath. All the joy of the welcome she had planned seemed to have gone. Uneasily she sensed trouble ahead.

Turk felt even more unjustly in disgrace at being shut in the tool-shed. He began to connect this with the coming of the strange dog. It did not help to pacify him when Nero rushed snapping at the small gap between the door and the step and yapped away impudently at him. Turk could only put his nose down to the gap and growl in frustration. Mrs Jarvis shook her head sadly at Dr Jarvis and muttered, "This can't go on."

That night when the rest of the family was in bed she and the doctor quietly discussed the trouble. "What's to happen,

John? We can't shut Flash up every time Nero is let out."

"Maybe in time they'll settle down together. I agree it was an unfortunate beginning."

"The children are resentful, though, and I did want us to be a happy family."

"After all, there is some reason in their attitude. Flash is their dog and this is Flash's home," Dr Jarvis pointed out.

"But Mother *did* ask if she could bring her dog and we agreed. He's been her companion for about four years now and she's grown very fond of him. After all, Flash is just a stray dog and he's only been here about six weeks."

"Do you think I should hand him over to the police as a stray, then? I am afraid that would only antagonise the children even more and make them feel unfriendly towards their grandmother."

"Oh dear! I don't know what to think." Mrs Jarvis was almost on the verge of tears herself. "It's true the children have got fond of Flash, especially Susan."

"Just try to keep the dogs separate for a few days till they've got accustomed to the sight and smell of each other. Flash isn't a quarrelsome dog. I don't think he'll go for Nero if Nero doesn't aggravate him."

"I'm not so sure of Nero." Mrs Jarvis shook her head.

"How would it be if Susan took Nero for a walk on the leash each day? She's good with dogs. Your mother is too lame to walk the dog herself and she'd be pleased at Susan offering to do it," Dr Jarvis suggested. "Susan might grow fond of Nero too and if it came to a separation from Flash, she'd take it less badly."

"I'll have a word with Susan," Mrs Jarvis promised.

"You can tell the children that the Manchester conference has been postponed and I'll take them and Flash for a run on the hills to compensate," Dr Jarvis decided.

So, for the next few days Susan took Nero on the leash

through the streets of Orrell and he became quite biddable and attached to her. Grandma Mackay was mollified and Turk was left at peace in the garden. His leg was strong again now and the garden was not enough. He grew restless and longed for freedom. He dreamed of the sheep on the soft green turf of the faraway hills. With the longing grew the urge again to find his old master, David Murray. Dogs do not forget easily.

The following Saturday Dr Jarvis kept his promise. "How would you like a run up to Rivington Pike?" he asked Peter and Susan. Rivington Pike was a high hill a few miles north of Wigan, not quite a mountain. All about it lay the rolling moors, Withnell, Anglezarke, Smithills, crowned with heather and dotted with sheep. From the highest point of Winter's Hill one could see Liverpool in the far distance to the south. Deep gullies clothed in ferns were cut down the hillsides by many streams. Here and there on Anglezarke Moor were old adits to lead mines long ago worked out. Now the entrances were blocked by stone or rotting timber.

Dr Jarvis took the road through the villages of Adlington and Rivington, then up a narrow road that wound steeply up the moor almost to the crest of Winter's Hill. Autumn was beginning and the slopes were tawny with bracken and the heather had faded to a dusty brown. Turk sat on the back seat between Peter and Susan. As soon as they reached the moors he began to tremble with excitement and to look from side to side through the back window. This was the kind of country he knew. He sniffed the air through the open window and it smelt of the moorland and sheep. He thumped his tail up and down with joy and whined with eagerness to get out.

"Mr Muir said Flash was a country dog. I think he's right," Peter remarked.

"I'll pull up on this level stretch and we'll all get out and let Turk have a scamper," Dr Jarvis told them.

At first Peter and Susan ran up and down with Turk on a leash till they were breathless but Turk was still fresh and eager.

"I think you can let Flash off the leash. He can't get into mischief here and there's no traffic to bother him," Dr Jarvis said.

Turk stood for a moment in unbelievable delight when the leash was unclipped from his collar. He was free! He could run where he liked over these sweet-smelling hills. He rushed in circles round the children, bounding with delight. He stopped and sniffed hard. It was there again, the familiar unforgettable smell of *sheep*. All the old instincts rose in him and he sped away to a small flock grazing on the shoulder of the hill.

"Come back, Flash!" Dr Jarvis cried, and he waved his arm towards himself in a circle. The doctor's was not the voice that once commanded Turk when he rounded up sheep, but Turk saw the arm waved in a circle. That had been one of the signs that he had to go round the sheep and bring them in. He had not forgotten it. Some of his old speed came back to him as he curved in a great arc to come in behind the sheep. They scented him and felt, rather than heard, his approach, and bunched themselves together. Cunningly, crouching behind them, stopping and starting, running from side to side, Turk began to urge the sheep across the moor towards the Jarvis family.

"Good gracious! Flash is fetching the sheep to us!" Dr Jarvis exclaimed.

"He must have been a sheep-dog on a farm," Peter declared.

They watched with surprise and interest the skilled way Turk rounded up the flock and brought them along without any fuss. The sheep had nearly reached them when an angry voice shouted behind them, "What do you mean by letting your dog harry my sheep?" There stood a farmer with a gun across his left shoulder and a stick in his right hand.

Dr Jarvis was quite taken aback. "He's not really *harrying* them. I think he's just rounding them up."

"And what right has he got to do that? What right have you to interfere with *my* sheep? I say he's harrying them and the next thing he'll be worrying them. Don't you know that farmers have a right to shoot strange dogs they find worrying their sheep?"

Dr Jarvis felt it was time he made a firm stand. "Our dog is *not* worrying your sheep."

"He hasn't even nipped a single one of them," Susan cried indignantly. There was a hint of fear in her voice too at the threat of Flash being shot.

"He's interfering with them and that's enough for me," the farmer declared angrily. "Call him off at once and think yourselves lucky I haven't fired at him."

"Flash! Flash, come here!" both the children shouted at once.

Turk heard the command and took his eyes off the flock for a brief moment. Two sheep broke loose and dashed away across the moor with Turk at their heels. All at once they disappeared entirely from view and Turk after them.

"The dog'll have driven them into a gully. They'll be lucky if their legs are not broken among the boulders. I tell you, mister, you'll pay for those sheep if they're damaged." The farmer was furious.

A frantic baaing and barking came from the gully, then the two sheep emerged unhurt, but in a panic. Turk appeared behind them and then he sent them cantering over the moor to join the remainder of the flock. He rushed back to the gully and disappeared again.

"Now where's he gone?" Dr Jarvis demanded, exasperated.

From down the gully came the sound of peremptory barking. The Jarvis family and the farmer rushed towards the steep gully opening like a deep crack in the hillside.

"Careful now!" Dr Jarvis cried, restraining his children. "We don't want any broken bones."

Below them the gully fell away steeply to a small stream

bestrewn with boulders. There at the bottom stood Turk, barking up at them. At his feet a young sheep lay on her back, wedged between boulders, her legs waving in the air as she struggled feebly to get up. Turk was urging her to greater efforts by barking close to her.

The farmer put down his gun and with the stick he climbed cautiously down the gully followed by Dr Jarvis. "You children stay on top," he ordered them. They peered anxiously over the rim of the gully between the fronds of ferns to see what happened. The farmer reached the sheep first. "Away, you!" he shouted at Turk, then struck him a blow with his stick that caught Turk in the ribs. Turk gave a howl of pain and retreated a yard up the gully. The farmer raised his stick threateningly again.

"Steady on, there!" Dr Jarvis shouted to the farmer. "You've no call to strike my dog. He's just found your sheep for you."

"Found it! The way he was harrying those sheep there's no doubt he drove it down here first," Farmer Anderton retorted.

"He did *not*!" Peter yelled from above. "Only two sheep ran away from the flock. *That* sheep must have been there all the time. Flash found him for you. You ought to be jolly grateful to him."

"Cheeky young pup!" Farmer Anderton shouted back.

Peter might have retorted but his father said, "That's enough, Peter!" Although he had checked his son, he told the farmer in cold anger, "The boy's right. We saw only *two* sheep go down into the gully and the dog brought them out again. This one must have been here some time. Look at his weak condition."

Anderton grunted but said no more. He was beginning to think Peter and the doctor were right and to regret losing his temper. He felt the sheep, and the animal was feeble and half dead with cold, its coat soaking wet. It had not rained since the previous night. Anderton realised the sheep must have been lying on its back in the gully for some time. Another few hours and it would have died.

"I'm sorry if I lost my temper and struck the dog," he told Dr Jarvis. "Give me a hand to shift these boulders and get the sheep on her feet again."

Together they lifted the boulders wedging in the sheep, then the farmer gave a powerful heave and the sheep stood on her feet again. The animal panted with fright and still stood as though rooted to the spot. "Up you go!" the farmer said, tapping the ewe with his stick, but she stumbled and almost collapsed for her legs were weak and cramped with cold.

"Aye, I think that sheep has lain in the gully overnight," Anderton apologised to the doctor. "I'll have to carry her up to the top. Will you take my stick up, please?"

With the doctor assisting over the steeper places the farmer struggled to the top with the sheep. He set it down well away from the edge and immediately it began to munch at the grass. The farmer began to urge it towards the rest of the flock in the mid-distance, but the sheep was either too feeble or reluctant to take more than a few steps.

"We could do with your dog now to make this sheep stir her stumps a bit more," the farmer said. "Has he been a sheep-dog?"

"That we don't know." The doctor explained the circumstances that had made them adopt Turk. "He seems to know what to do with sheep."

"That's true. Whistle him up and I'll put him to driving this sheep back to the others."

"Where's Flash?" Dr Jarvis called to the children.

"He's not with us," Susan said. "We haven't seen him since he headed up the gully. Is he still there?"

Dr Jarvis whistled and called "Flash! Flash!" but there was no answering call from Turk, otherwise Flash. No scampering dog appeared.

"Where's he gone?" Dr Jarvis cried, bewildered. He went back to the gully and looked over the edge but there was no sign of the dog. The children shouted "Flash! Flash!" too, but there was no response.

"Wait here," Dr Jarvis told Peter and Susan. "I'll go down into the gully and look for him."

"I'll come with you," Farmer Anderton offered.

"Can we come too?" Peter asked.

"We'll be quicker by ourselves," the doctor said. "You stay there in case Flash comes back." He was beginning to worry lest the dog had fallen and was perhaps lying dead in some deep cleft. He and the farmer descended cautiously, and the farmer began to beat about with his stick in the ferny hollows while Dr Jarvis searched the pools along the little stream. There was no sign of Turk. At last, after they had searched the gully thoroughly, they had to give up.

"He's not here." Dr Jarvis shook his head. "He must have run away across the moor."

With the children they ranged over part of the moor calling "Flash! Flash!" but got no response. The sun was beginning to drop low in the sky. The children were tired out and Susan was weepy.

"We can't search the whole of Rivington Pike before dark," Dr Jarvis decided.

"That's true. There are at least a dozen steep gullies between here and Brinscall where the dog might be lying and it'll soon be too dark to see him," Farmer Anderton agreed.

At this blunt unfortunate remark Susan burst into tears.

"Now, lassie, don't cry," the farmer said in a kindly voice. "Maybe the dog's just gone rabbiting and he'll turn up tomorrow morning watching the sheep, if he's a sheep-dog.

Sheep-dogs are hardy and a night on the moors won't hurt him. I'll keep a look-out for him and if I see him in the morning I'll collar him and take him to the farm." He turned to Dr Jarvis. "If you'll give me your phone number I'll give you a call tomorrow if I find him."

The two men exchanged names, addresses and phone numbers.

"Come along now, children. It's my turn to be on call duty tonight so we'll have to go back at once."

Susan burst into tears again but Peter knew how important it was that his father should be ready to answer any urgent summons. "Someone might be very ill and want Daddy in a hurry," he reminded Susan. Reluctantly the children got into the car and Dr Jarvis drove away.

When Turk received the whack from Farmer Anderton he was furiously angry too. Only the patient kind discipline he had been taught by old David Murray prevented him from going for the farmer. Turk had expected praise for finding the sheep, not a harsh blow. He ran away up the gully. While everyone's attention was fixed on the exhausted sheep Turk turned up another side gully and scrambled out among bushes on the far side away from the children. He sped across the turf and away among the heather. Soon he smelt out new trails, rabbit tracks, hares, old nests of peewits, golden plovers and grouse: all the lovely interesting scents of the moors that he had known so well. He ran further and further across the moor of Anglezarke away from the gully, his nose to the ground, following this trail and that. The shouts of Dr Jarvis and the children were faint and far away and Turk did not heed them. Once more he was tasting strange heady freedom and the moors called to him. He followed the scent of a rabbit. All at once it was crossed by another scent, that of a stoat. Stoats were old enemies. The hairs on Turk's neck bristled. He knew the stoat was pursuing a rabbit for its scent had overlain the rabbit's. Both were fresh scents and neither of the small animals could be far away. Nose to the ground Turk went slinking after them through the heather and turf. No longer did the shouts of the Jarvis family reach him: he was too far away now, too interested in following his prey.

The trail led to a bank overlooking another gully. The bank was a rabbit warren. Turk was just in time to see the bushy brown tail of the stoat disappearing into the burrow and to hear the terrified squeal of the rabbit as the stoat sunk his teeth in it. It's a brave dog which will tackle a stoat in a narrow space but Turk did not hesitate. He grabbed hold of the stoat's tail with his teeth and dragged him backwards out of the hole, the stoat hanging on to the young rabbit and pulling it with him. Once outside, the stoat let go the rabbit and faced his attacker. He sprang to sink his fangs in Turk's throat but Turk was too quick for him and leaped aside and dealt the stoat a blow with his paw that sent him rolling on the turf. The stoat was up on his feet in a second and came again at Turk with bared teeth, just as Turk made to attack him. This time the stoat's teeth grazed Turk's muzzle but he failed to get a hold. The scratch made Turk more wary. He backed a yard or so, jumping from left to right and back again continuously so as to confuse the stoat but he never took his eyes off those gleaming fangs in that cruel mouth.

Suddenly the stoat made a dart at him but Turk was ready for it. He leaped aside and the stoat just missed his throat by an inch. As the stoat wheeled about, Turk pounced. He gripped him by the furry ruff all stoats have. Turk sank his teeth deep and though the stoat wriggled and fought, Turk held on. He never let go his grip though the stoat tried to scratch at his eyes. Then he began to shake the stoat. To and fro, back and forth, Turk shook him in that relentless grip. The stoat

began to go dizzy. Turk wiped him back and forth on the
ground, sorely mauling the lithe body. The stoat's wriggling
grew more and more feeble. At last Turk gave the stoat a
tremendous swing against a stone and his back was broken.
The little animal gave a hissing sigh and went limp. Slowly
Turk relaxed his grip and the stoat's body slid to the ground.
Turk turned it over with a cautious paw. He did not risk his
muzzle near those needle-like teeth in case the stoat was
foxing dead. The body rolled over and did not stir. The stoat
was dead right enough. Turk turned his attention to the
rabbit.

It was lying with glazed eyes, dead too. Turk's onslaught
on the stoat had come too late to save it. The stoat's teeth had
pierced an artery in its neck. Turk nosed it too and rolled
it over, not knowing quite what to do with it. When he had
gone rabbiting at Glenbield he had sometimes carried a dead
rabbit back in his mouth to the farm. He lifted the rabbit
now, gently, between his teeth, but there was no one to whom
he could take it. He looked about him, not knowing quite
what to do, then he set the rabbit down again. He sat down,
keeping his eyes on the dead rabbit and stoat, waiting, listening for the familiar whistle.

The sun went down in a blaze of glory and the dusk began
to gather on the moor. There was a whirr of wings and out
of the sky a feathered form pounced on the stoat and carried
it off. It was the stoat's ancient enemy, the owl. Turk
snatched up the rabbit again. This was *his* prize now: no
enemy bird should take it from him. Suddenly he realised
he was hungry. It was his usual supper time. He wandered
over the moor, going ever northward, looking for a place
where he might devour the rabbit in peace.

He found it at last. It was an opening between rocks,
partly concealed by a broken door. Round about were heaps
of rocky shale overgrown by nettles and willow herb—the

willow herb that always springs up where once men have lived or worked. Turk put down the rabbit and thrust his head into the opening. A stone rolled down inside the hole, falling with a hollow plop somewhere below. There was no other sound. Turk explored a little further, sniffing here and there. The only scent was a very faint one of man, a scent of long ago. Immediately inside the hole was a square slab of stone like a big step. Turk took the rabbit in with him and lay upon the slab, his face to the opening. There he made his supper of the rabbit, obeying the law of the wild. He was hungry and the rabbit was his lawful meat by right of his battle with the stoat. At last, satisfied, and after sniffing round for possible enemies, with one ear alert, he curled up on the stone and fell asleep at the adit to the old lead mine. It was an uneasy sleep, haunted by dreams of Glenbield. He woke at dawn with a hunger upon him, not a hunger for meat but for those far northern hills. He gave a whimper and a yawn, rose and stretched himself, forward and backward, and sniffed the air of the morning. Instinct was right. It was *north* he must go to seek his hills of home. He went down to the little stream, lapped the water thirstily, then pointed his muzzle towards the north and whined. That was the way he must go. He set off at a steady pace that ate up the miles. By the time Farmer Anderton was awake Turk was already following the stream towards the reservoirs on the northern side of Rivington Pike, many miles away.

When Dr Jarvis rang Mr Anderton next day the farmer had no news for him. "I was out early with my own dog but we saw nothing of yours. Of course he might have left the moor and gone down to one of the villages at the hill foot. I'll make enquiries there."

"Thank you, Mr Anderton."

"He'll have your name and address on his collar, of course?"

"Well—er—no. I only got the collar recently and I had no time to wait while it was engraved. I've been very busy as one of my partners in the practice has been ill." The doctor sounded regretful. The two children were standing beside him at the telephone, hoping to hear that Flash had been found.

"Oh, Daddy!" Susan cried despairingly.

"I'll give you a call if I hear any news," the farmer promised. Dr Jarvis thanked him and rang off.

"I'm sorry, Susan. I ought to have seen to Flash's name being engraved," Dr Jarvis said contritely. "We'll keep in touch with the villages around Rivington Pike. Meanwhile, perhaps Grandma will let you take out Nero for walks."

"Nero's awfully spoilt. He's not a bit as nice-tempered as Flash," Susan lamented.

"He's better than no dog at all," Peter tried to console her. "Besides, perhaps Flash might come back yet," he added; but he was doubtful.

The days went by and the Jarvis family heard no more of 'Flash', who was Turk. He never did come back and in time Nero took his place in Susan's affections. They did not know that Flash was steadily pursuing a dream, his nose pointing northwards—a dream that was to lead him into strange adventures.

Turk set off at a steady pace along the ridge of Withnell Moor. Now and again he paused and lifted his nose and sniffed the wind. It came from the north-west and blew the first autumn leaves scurrying before it. Turk went downhill and soon reached a narrow road that ran alongside a reservoir. The deep water was uninviting and Turk could see no fish so he turned away to the lower ground to the north of the moors. He passed clusters of houses along a railway. To the north-east rose the smoke of thousands of chimneys in the town of Blackburn. To Turk smoke meant many houses and busy roads with terrifying traffic. He cut down into a stretch of woodland that seemed promising.

He was beginning to feel thirsty after his long run and he could smell water. He nosed about and came to the edge of the wood. There lay the water before him, a winding stretch of the Leeds and Liverpool Canal. Turk bounded towards it, then came to a headlong stop too late. His feet skidded on the muddy towpath and he hurtled straight into the canal.

In a moment he had surfaced and was swimming. He swallowed some of the muddy water and slaked his thirst, then made for the opposite bank. It was a high stone embankment almost three feet above him. Turk tried to leap up on to it but it is very hard to leap from water where there is nothing to give the feet a grip. He scrabbled with his paws at the smooth stones of the embankment but he could gain no purchase. He swam along the canal trying to find a gap in the wall above him but there was no gap. He tried his luck on the other side of the canal but that was equally unscalable. Turk swam up and down desperately trying to find a foothold somewhere. He was beginning to tire and his swimming paddle became more feeble. The canal took a big bend. With a great effort he swam towards it.

Suddenly the sharp sound of a siren smote on his ears. A great black object was bearing down upon him. His frightened ears remembered the fire-engine and the cars. He tried to get out of the way but the motor-barge came slowly, inexorably on, towing another barge in its wake. He was in danger of being crushed between the barge and the canal wall. Again the siren warned him to get clear. With a last frantic effort he swam across its bows to the clear stretch of water on the other side. The barge, *The Pride of Leeds*, pulled slowly alongside; the motor stopped and the barge began to lose way. A silence fell over the canal save for the lapping water as the barge drifted on. A man leaned out from the motor house and spotted Turk paddling desperately to keep afloat.

"There's a dog in the water. It seems at its last gasp. Can you hook it out as we pass?" he shouted to his wife in the butty-boat behind.

She seized the ever-handy boat-hook. "Aye, Tom!" she shouted back. She bent over the side of the barge and with unerring precision thrust the boat-hook under Turk's collar and drew him towards the barge. This was even more terrifying to Turk who yelped in a panic.

"He's a right heavy dog. I can't lift him clean out with the hook," she shouted to her husband.

"Hold on! I'll come over to you," he cried, and jumped out of the barge and ran along the towpath.

"Bring him round the stern to the towpath, Kate," he directed his wife.

She dragged Turk through the water spluttering and choking, round the stern and to the canal bank, and pushed him close to it. Turk floundered in a panic of fear. Tom lay on the towpath and put out an arm at full stretch and grabbed hold of Turk's collar and lifted.

"By gum! He's some weight of a dog!" Tom said as Turk flopped exhausted beside him.

"He looks fair done to me," Kate said as her husband scrambled to his feet again. "He's a bonnie-looking dog even if he's soaked to the skin. My! How he's shivering! Here! Lift him aboard and let's see what I can do for him."

Tom put him on the little deck on the stern of the butty-boat. Turk took several deep breaths, then stumbled to his feet and shook himself violently.

"Hi, you! Don't drown me!" Kate laughed. She reached a spare sack from the front of the butty-boat and began to rub Turk down. He stood still while she dried off his soaking coat as best she could. He was still trembling with cold and the terror he had just escaped.

"The poor beast'll be the better for something hot to eat. I've got stew on the stove," she said, and jumped down a couple of steps into the tiny galley. A stewpan stood on a small calor-gas cooking stove. She ladled a generous quantity into a bowl.

"Eh, lass! Don't be giving the dog *my* share!" Tom laughed.

"You've not been in the cut," she told him in her good Lancashire voice, "so you're not needing it the same!"

She let the stew cool down, then she set it before Turk. Turk needed no second invitation. Though it was still hot he lapped it up eagerly.

"I bet you've given him all the meat," Tom declared. "Eh,

there never was such a lass for spoiling childer and animals."
He looked at his stout wife with teasing affection all the same.
Sharp of tongue she might be, but she had a heart of gold. . . .

"Well, we've got no bairns aboard nowadays," Kate said
with a sigh. "They grow up too fast. Since our Joe got his own
narrow-boat and got married, it's been kind of lonely without
him. And with Jeff in Canada, goodness knows when we'll
ever see him again! And our Nelly's thronged with work and
babies on Bob's farm. She's a right good farmer's wife,
though, but times I wish I could change places with her and
have my childer all over again." All this time she was stroking
and patting Turk as he ate. Turk put out a quick tongue and
licked her hand. "See that? He kissed me. How's that for a
dumb beast saying 'Thank you' for his meat?"

"Aye, he's a well-mannered dog right enough," Tom
agreed.

"It's a long time since we had old Toby. I sometimes think
we could do with a dog on the boat, Tom. A good watch-dog
would be a protection against those young vandals in some
towns."

Tom knew what was coming. "No doubt! But this one
belongs to someone else. Let's have a look at the name on his
collar." To his surprise there was no name. "Well now, that's
a queer-like thing," he said. "That looks a new collar but
there's no name in it."

"Then we don't know who owns him." There was a hint
of triumph in Kate's voice.

"I suppose not, but we could hand him over to the police
in the next town," Tom suggested.

"A fat lot of good that would do! The police won't know
who he belongs to either. Besides, we're behind time with this
cargo already. You'll be later still if you go rooting round to
find the police and to fill up a lot of papers. No, lad, I'll tell
you what we'll do. We'll leave word about the dog with the

lock-keepers and the pubs along the cut. They'll know to find him aboard the *Pride of Leeds* if anyone claims him."

"I can see you're bent on having him," Tom grinned.

"Oh, Tom, there are times I'm proper lonely when you're in front all day wi' the motor-boat and I'm alone in t' butty. I could do wi' a bit of company," Kate sighed.

"It's no use saying 'no', I can see." Tom's voice was indulgent. "You've always had your own way."

"And most of the time I've been right, too," Kate said briskly. "You can't deny that. Well, he's stopping on the *Pride of Leeds* and you'll maybe be glad of him if we run up against a gang of young toughs."

"You'll need to tie him up till he's got used to us, or he'll be skipping off at the next set of locks," Tom said practically.

"A bit of rope'll do till I find Toby's old leash," she said. "There's a good-sized piece here that I used to hitch on to Nell's little lad to keep him from falling overboard. That'll give the dog plenty of freedom to move round the deck and into the cabin."

"By gum, then, you'd better teach the poor beast to wipe his feet before he comes into your cabin!" Tom chuckled.

Kate's cabin was a model of spotless cleanliness and famed throughout the fleet of narrow-boats on the canal.

"Well, we'd best get moving again but I hope you never meet an elephant that needs care or I'll have to buy a liner." He swung off back to the motor-boat and Kate hitched the rope through Turk's collar. As the boat began to move again she swung the tiller of the butty-boat. Turk was surprised and restless at first to see the land slipping past him. Soon, however, he crouched at Kate's feet. The warm food inside him and the drowsy motion of the boat sent him to sleep.

He was awakened by some slight commotion aboard. They had arrived at Lock 57 at the Nova Scotia locks in the heart of Blackburn. Tom shouted to Kate who jumped on to the towpath carrying a long peculiar-shaped iron handle. This was the "key" to the lock gates. She inserted it in a hole in the great wooden doors across the canal and began to turn it like a winch. The doors began to open. Tom edged the motor-boat into the lock. The butty-boat swung after it. From the towpath Kate handled the towrope adroitly and brought the butty-boat alongside the motor-boat. Once the two boats were inside the lock Kate worked the handle that closed the doors again. The two boats lay in the narrow, enclosed space.

Turk looked up at the high stone walls of the lock with misgiving. Every outdoor animal has a horror of being in an enclosed space from which there is no escape. He whined and looked anxiously for Kate whom he knew instinctively was his friend. She reappeared looking over the top of the upper lock gates. Again she wielded the "key" and the big wooden doors opened slowly. From the widening gap a torrent of water began to pour into the lock. It boiled and surged round the two boats as they bobbed up and down. Turk was terrified. He felt trapped in the narrow lock with the water surging in whirlpools about them. He barked on a high-pitched note of fear and strained on the rope that tethered him to try to get away as far as he could from the upper lock gates. He could only retreat as far as the butty-boat stern deck. He let out a piteous howl. Kate looked down on him from the height of the lock. "It's all right, lad!" she called. "There's naught to be frightened of. I'll be back with you in a minute."

Turk grew calmer, reassured by her voice, though he continued to tremble. Then he had another surprise. The sides of the lock seemed to be moving downwards! Really the boats were rising with the lift of the water under them. Soon once more the sides of the narrow-boats were level with the towpath running alongside the lock. Kate jumped aboard again and took the tiller. Turk leaped up to greet her, licking her hand.

"You're a right softie," Kate said indulgently, laughing at him. "It's plain you've never been on a narrow-boat before. Eh, well, you'll learn." She stooped and patted him. The boats began to move slowly out of the lock. The motor-boat led the way on to the level stretch of the canal. On either side were the tall, grim walls of factories and warehouses closing in on the canal like a canyon. Turk looked up at them unhappily. Where were the green fields and the moors? The walls hemmed him in with the horror of a nightmare. He whined pleadingly at Kate. "We'll soon be out of this, lad," she told him, understanding his fear. There were still two other locks through which they had to go.

Kate looked doubtfully at Turk as they approached the second lock. "You were frightened, left aboard by yourself. This time I'll take you with me," she said. She opened a drawer in the cabin and took out a leash. "I'll put old Toby's leash on you, lad." She unhitched the rope and snapped on the leash. Turk quivered with delight. He had grown to recognise a leash as heralding a walk. When the two boats stopped below the lock gates and Kate leaped ashore he gladly leaped with her. Once they were ashore Kate hitched his leash round the leather belt that she wore so she had both hands for the job of opening the lock gates and then guiding the butty-boat in alongside the motor-boat. Turk paused when she paused, trotting alongside her. From the top gates he looked over the side and watched the lock filling and the boats rising. It did not seem so fearful now he was on firm ground beside Kate. She stooped and patted him. "It's not so bad now you know, is it?" she said with ready understanding.

They reached the third lock. This time Turk knew what was to happen and he gave a yap of delight when Kate jumped on to the towpath with him. Tom watched them with amusement. "You'll be training him to do the job for you next, lass."

"The poor creature likes a bit of a change, same as me," she retorted. "Sometimes I think all the change *I* get is when I work the locks."

Turk seemed reluctant to go aboard again. He strained slightly at the leash and gave an inviting bark at Kate. He really wanted to be let off the leash, but Kate did not understand that.

"I think he wants me to take him for a walk," she told Tom. "You pull ahead with the boats. It's a straight stretch for a mile so you'll manage without me in the butty-boat. I'll give him a run along the towpath."

"Aye, he'll need a run ashore now and again for his own needs. He seems to have had training in clean ways but it will be as well to get him used to the same ways on the boat."

"I was thinking that, too," Kate said. "Wait for us just before you reach the bridge."

Tom was rather glad his wife had taken the dog aboard He knew she missed their son Joe very much and when Toby, their dog, had died of old age, she had fretted. This new dog seemed to have brought back her usual cheerful spirit.

"Come for a walk, then, lad?" Kate asked Turk, and he jumped up and down on all fours with delight. He was disappointed, though, when she did not take him off the leash. He had expected to run free, but he trotted along obediently, suiting his pace to hers. Now and again she slowed down to let him nose among the fences and walls. The scents he found there were strange ones; scents of other dogs, but no sheepdogs. Above all he missed the scent of sheep. Instead there were the smells of industry, raw cotton, cotton-seed oil, engine grease, diesel fumes, smoke from factory chimneys, all

alien to his nostrils. The heart-ache for the hills grew strong in him.

They reached the waiting boats and went aboard again. Tom started off again as soon as they were aboard. Once more Kate took the tiller to swing the butty-boat round the bends. Turk sat, half-dozing as he watched the landscape slip by.

Suddenly their peaceful progress was shattered. A tin-can full of small stones crashed on deck, narrowly missing Kate at the tiller. Another stone was flung at Turk. He jumped up, barking furiously. Four boys about twelve years old were leaning over the parapet of the bridge yelling at them with jeering laughter. Kate shook her fist at them. "You young limbs of Satan! Just let me get hold of you!"

"You can't touch us up here, missus!" one boy taunted her, putting his tongue out.

"Can't I? You'll see!" she shouted back. Quick as thought she unhitched the rope from Turk's collar. "After 'em, lad! Drive them off!" she cried.

Turk understood. He was to go after the boys as if they were sheep. Kate had used the word "Drive!" and pointed at the boys. He needed no second command. He bounded on to the towpath and up the sloping ramp to the bridge. The boys let go their hold on the parapet, slid down and began to run.

Kate blew hard on a whistle to signal Tom to stop. He did so at once, though the way on the boats took them another few yards, then they drifted into the curving bank of the canal. Tom leaped ashore. "What's up?" he shouted.

Kate came puffing up to him, brandishing the lock key she had snatched up. "It's those young rascals of lads on that bridge. They're at their old tricks of throwing things at the butty-boat as we come up to the bridge. It's the same bad lot of boys that did it before. I've sent the dog to chase them."

The boys took to their heels but they could not out-distance Turk. He went at the same terrific speed that he did on an out-run with the sheep. He caught up with the boys but to their surprise he passed them by. Obeying his old training for rounding up sheep he made a quick turn and came back again to face them. The astonished boys backed away. Just behind them was the narrow approach to the bridge. It reminded Turk of the gates through which he had to drive his sheep. He crouched down, keeping his eye upon the lads and began to slink towards them as if about to pounce. The power of his eye almost held them as if they *were* sheep. They took fright at this strange dog, panicked and ran for the end of the bridge, Turk after them. He pretended to snap at their heels but his early training prevented him from biting them. He kept the boys in a bunch and if one tried to break away Turk quickly pounced in his direction. Down the ramp they ran and on to the towpath, towards the boats, not knowing where to turn to get away from the pursuing dog. Tom and Kate stared in amazement. The boys were running towards them with Turk hot on their heels.

"Jings!" Tom exclaimed. "The dog's rounded them up!"

The boys flung themselves at Tom. "Call off your dog, mister!"

Unaware that she was still holding it, Kate was brandishing the lock key. "Oh, missus, please let us off!" the boys implored her.

"Down, lad!" she called to Turk.

Turk immediately crouched behind the group of boys and held them in front of Tom and Kate.

"Let us off this time, mister, and we won't throw stones at your boat any more," a boy pleaded.

"I'll take good care you don't!" Tom declared. "This isn't the first time you've done it but it'll be the last! Get aboard with you!"

"Oh, no, mister!" The boys were dithering with fright.

"On board!" Tom was inflexible. Kate flourished her lock key. "Quick, now, or I'll set the dog on you," she threatened. Little did they know that Turk would never have bitten any of them, any more than he would have bitten a sheep!

Thoroughly cowed, the boys reluctantly stepped aboard the *Pride of Leeds*. Kate followed them and Turk jumped aboard after her.

"Watch them, lad!" Kate ordered him. Turk recognised that command too. He crouched before the boys, ready to jump if one made a move.

"What are you going to do with us, mister?" one of the boys called to Tom who was watching them from the tow-path.

"Teach you a lesson you'll not forget!" Tom told them grimly. "You'll see! You're going for a trip with me and don't try jumping off or you'll find yourselves in the cut, if the dog doesn't get you first!"

Kate guessed her husband's intention and though she kept a straight face, she was chuckling inwardly. Tom started the engine and the motor-boat moved away from the bank. Kate gave one practised swing at the tiller of the butty-boat and the space between it and the bank increased quickly. It was much too wide for the boys to jump. "Sit on the deck!" she ordered. "Watch them, dog!" Turk stood guard.

For a mile the two narrow-boats progressed in silence, then one of the boys asked, "Where are you taking us, missus?"

"It'll be a surprise for you," she told him.

"You're . . . you're not taking us all the way to Leeds, are you, missus? If . . . if I'm not home for my tea I'll get a hiding from my mother," the smallest boy told her tearfully.

"That might do you good," was Kate's reply.

The oldest boy was bolder. "If you take us to Leeds we'll put the police on to you."

"I wouldn't have too much to say about the police if I was you," Kate quenched him. "You might find yourself at a police station."

All the time Turk stayed in one position, never taking his eyes off the boys.

"I don't like the way that dog stares at us all the time," one boy muttered.

"You're lucky he only *stares*!" was Kate's retort. "Better keep your tongue still!"

There was silence after that for the next mile. The boys began to look more and more anxious and subdued. The barges went through a long tunnel beneath the railway and a hill, the Foulridge Tunnel. The boys stirred restlessly and began to mutter. Turk did not like the darkness either, nor the sound of the boat's wash lapping against the sides of the tunnel. He growled in protest, but his growl quietened the boys again.

"No use trying to jump off here! The dog's watching," Kate warned them. She was beginning to feel rather sorry for the boys and wondered just what Tom intended to do with them.

At the village of Rishton the canal took a sharp turn to the south to avoid the higher land to the north. The canal ran alongside the main road for a few hundred yards. Tom drew the motor-boat into the bank and stopped. He came along to the butty-boat. "Now, lads," he said to the boys. "The next lock is near to a police station. I could hand you over there and leave the police to deal with you." He paused and the boys looked at him with apprehension. "I'm going to give you another chance, though, but if ever you fling another stone or a tin-can at a canal barge, I'll be there before you can say 'knife!'"

"We'll never do it again, mister," a boy promised.

"Right! Well, yon's the main road from Accrington to Blackburn. You can walk it back again now. It'll be four or five miles. 'Appen it'll give you an appetite for your tea, if your mothers save you any. You'll need to hurry, for it'll be dark by the time you get back. Let 'em go, dog!"

The boys needed no second bidding. They jumped ashore in such a hurry that one of them fell to his knees on the towpath. Turk stood and barked at them, but Kate had taken the precaution of snapping the leash on him quickly lest he should chase them. The boys sprinted their fastest from the towpath to the road.

"I bet they run all the way back to Blackburn," Tom chuckled with satisfaction.

"The dog's done his share," Kate said, fondling Turk, "I told you he'd be a good watch-dog."

"Aye, he rounded up those kids as if they'd been sheep," Tom laughed, then added thoughtfully, "I wonder if he *has* been a sheep-dog? I've seen sheep farmers with dogs like him."

"Maybe, but without him we couldn't have handled those boys the way we did." She patted Turk. "Good lad! There'll be something extra for your supper tonight."

After a few days Turk soon fell into the routine of canal-boat life. He liked being on deck beside Kate as she worked the tiller. He enjoyed his walk with her along the towpath morning and evening, even if she did keep him on a leash. Though Turk never really liked the locks he ceased to tremble and whine as the boats went through them. When the boats tied up at some wharf for the night he joined Kate and Tom in the warm cabin, sitting at their feet while Tom smoked his pipe and Kate was busy with her knitting. A month passed by and the *Pride of Leeds* made several trips between Liverpool and Leeds and back again. Turk seemed to settle well on the boat, but it was a lazy life for him.

"We've never been plagued with those bad lads at Blackburn again," Kate said complacently.

"No, I reckon the dog scared the living daylights out of
them," Tom chuckled.

"He seems to belong to us now. I wonder who owned him
before he joined us?" Kate paused in her knitting. "Look at
him asleep there. Every now and again his ears twitch and
sometimes he gives a little whimper. Do you think he's
dreaming?"

"Aye, they do say that dogs dream," Tom replied.

"I wonder what he dreams about?"

"Goodness knows, lass! Maybe dog-fights!"

But it was not of dog-fights that Turk dreamed. It was of
ranging wide and free over green pastures and heather moors
dotted with sheep and of returning only in answer to the
whistle of the one man he had loved most of all. Dogs have
long memories.

Tom and Kate had no idea of the homesick longing that Turk had for the hills of the north. Once or twice Kate had let Turk off the leash along the towpath but it had always been near a town where the canal wound between streets. To Turk streets meant noise and horrible traffic and he felt happier on the towpath, so he just ran ahead of Kate and kept coming back to her.

There was a chill in the autumn evenings and the darkness fell earlier. There was occasional hoar frost on the grass and bushes in the mornings which made the spiders' webs look like silver lace. Great gaggles of geese flew southward in wedge-shaped formations. Tom's daily journeys grew shorter as the hours of daylight grew fewer. Turk knew from all these signs that winter was nearing. Soon the ground would be hard with frost and covered with snow. There grew an urge in him to reach the Border hills while he could still race across them. Soon it would be time to gather in the flocks from the hills and bring them nearer to the homestead. Memories of flock-gathering stirred in Turk's mind. He felt he must be there.

Below Silsden just north of Keighley, the canal wound round the foot of Silsden Moor. The land rose steeply beyond to Ilkley Moor. The canal took a bend round a narrow patch of woodland. Tom had brought the boats to a standstill on this quiet stretch of the canal while he and Kate had break-fast in the butty-boat. The smells of the countryside drew Turk on deck. Dotted on Silsden Moor he could see and smell the sheep. He longed to run on the moors behind them and he pointed his nose skywards and whined.

"What ails you, lad?" Tom called to him from the cabin.

"He'll be wanting his walk," Kate said. "He knows it's time for it when we've finished breakfast."

"He keeps sniffing and pointing with his nose," Tom said. "I think he can smell rabbits in that woodland there. Perhaps he wants to go rabbiting."

"Well, I can't go rabbiting with him. There's a nasty barbed-wire fence round that stretch of woodland."

"Eh, he doesn't need you with him when he's going rabbiting, lass. You'd just be in his way. He'd be a lot quicker on his own."

"'Appen!" Kate agreed.

"A bit of rabbit pie would be right gradely," Tom observed. "I bet you he'd bring a rabbit back to us in his mouth. Let him have a go, Kate."

"What? Let him off the leash?"

"Aye, you've done it afore."

"But that was near streets," Kate pointed out.

"What difference does it make? He'll come back when you whistle."

"Well, all right . . ." Kate said rather reluctantly. She clipped the leash on Turk while they jumped ashore and she led him to the woodland, then took the leash off. She pointed to the woodland. "Fetch us a rabbit, lad."

Turk needed no second bidding. He crouched and wriggled under the barbed wire and into the wood. He was free, free to run where he liked! He gave sharp barks of joy and frisked about as he ran. He gave one or two sniffs: there were no rabbit scents but he could smell *sheep* on the moor.

In a couple of minutes he was through the wood, under the barbed wire on the far side and scrambling at top speed over the fells. He came to a narrow cross-roads and unerringly chose the one leading north to the High Moor. Soon he left the road which became little more than a narrow track and found himself ranging the high wide slopes of Ilkley Moor and looking down on the far side of it to the town of Ilkley.

His nose would have led him straight to the sheep but as he rounded a hillock he saw they were already in the charge of a shepherd with a big stick who had his own dog beside him. The other dog barked furiously as soon as Turk appeared. He might have gone for Turk but the shepherd said sternly, "Down, Brigg!" and the dog stopped at once. Turk stopped in mid-run too and the two dogs eyed each other. Then the farmer shook his stick at Turk. "Away, you!" he shouted.

Turk knew better than to interfere with a flock that was in charge of another dog. At once he turned about and ran over the crest of the hill and downwards to the valley on the other side while the shepherd muttered, "I wonder who that dog belongs to? Folk are a right nuisance that let their dogs run wild."

At the foot of the opposite side of the hill Kate was waiting for Turk to come back with a rabbit. She peered through the strands of barbed wire into the woodland and called and whistled for Turk. She walked down the towpath running alongside the wood in case Turk should be at the far end of the wood. There was neither sight nor sound of him. Tom, aboard the motor-boat, grew impatient to set off again and sounded the boat's siren as a signal for their return. Kate came running back.

"Tom, Tom! I've lost the dog. He went into the wood but he didn't come back when I whistled him. I can't get into the wood for the barbed wire."

"I'll have a go," Tom said. "You stay with the boats and sound the siren if he comes back any other way."

"You don't think he's got his leg in any trap, do you?" Kate was quite distressed.

"Him? No, he's got more sense." All the same, Tom decided to look round for any possible traps left by a poacher.

Twenty minutes later he came back to the boats. "The dog's not in the wood. I've looked everywhere and beaten the bushes with my stick. He must have nipped out on the other side and gone over the moor."

"You told me to let him loose. We'll just have to wait for him coming back," Kate said.

"You know we can't wait all day, lass. There's this load of raw cotton to be delivered on time at Leeds. I'll wait an hour but after that we'll have to push on. We've wasted enough time as it is. You wouldn't want me to lose my job with the canal company."

Tom looked through the wood again and even went a short distance up on the moor. Kate whistled and called till she was hoarse but no dog came scampering along the tow-path to the barges. At last, reluctantly, Tom cast off the mooring rope he had hitched round a post in the fence. "We'll need to go now, lass," he said.

"I know." Kate looked tearful.

"Cheer up, my wench! Our Nelly'll find you another dog when Bess at the farm has her litter. You know she promised you a pup."

"Aye, but I'd kind of taken to *that* dog. 'Appen he'll catch up with us somewhere along the cut," Kate said, unwilling to give up hope.

But Turk never did catch up with them.

As Turk ran down the hill he saw the town of Ilkley nestling in the valley below him and the River Wharfe running through it like a silver ribbon. Beyond the river valley the hills rose to the north, green and tawny, beckoning him on, but first he would have to cross the river. For a moment Turk was reminded of the canal and of Kate and Tom. He hesitated but already he had tasted the joy of running the hills again. A cool breeze from the north-west brought the scent of the moors to him. He knew that somewhere, up there beyond the hills, was the home he sought and the people remembered in his dreams, to whom he really belonged. The instinct to go and find them outweighed the thought of returning to the canal boat. On the hills there was freedom. This was his life.

Turk went at a gentle trot down the slopes of Ilkley Moor but bore away to the left, avoiding the streets of houses. He came to a railway. Just as he was about to dart across it, a strange and horrible monster came clanking round a bend dragging a string of trucks after it. Turk had never seen a railway engine before. He cowered among the gorse bushes on the embankment and trembled, but the strange creature rattled past and took no notice of him. All the same, Turk lay panting behind his cover for some time after the train had disappeared into the distance. Then, at last, he ventured across the line, his head down, going like an arrow. He scrambled up the opposite embankment and found he had to cross the main road along which a thin stream of traffic ran. Again he halted, undecided whether to turn back, but the scent of the river lay beyond the road. A gap occurred in the traffic and he scuttled across the road like a rabbit, through the fence on the opposite side and he was in the water-meadows among the cows. He took no notice of them for there had been cows on the farm in times past. The cows took little notice of him either.

He reached the river bank. It sloped gently down to the water and there was another easy slope on the opposite side.

Turk let himself down gently into the river and walked till the water reached his chest, then he began to dog-paddle, breasting the current. He reached the other side, scrambled out and shook himself vigorously, the drops flying off him like a shower of crystal beads. Then, leaving the River Wharfe behind him, he made due north for the hills again. He travelled at a steady trot except where the steep fells forced him to a slower pace. Now and again he had to cross the stony gully of a water-course. He was clever about this, winding his way down to it warily and smelling out the easiest way. Sometimes the channel was a dried-up water-course; sometimes there would be a running stream. Whenever he reached a stream he paused to drink. The thought of food did not worry him yet for it was at night that he had his main meal of the day. Sometimes the gully would be narrow enough for him to leap across it. The keen wind from the north blew over the moors and intoxicated him. Now and again he disturbed a curlew or a snipe and he chased after it till it winged its way well beyond his reach. He knew he could never catch it but the chasing was pure joy. Now and again he even chased a moving cloud shadow. Always, though, he turned back to his northerly course again, sniffing the wind for his direction. The evening shadows were lying long across the fells before he flagged. Even then it was the necessity to find food and a place to sleep for the night that halted him.

It was beginning to rain. Although it was easy to shake the drops from his coat after a dip in the river, it was not so easy to shake off the rain when it continued to fall. Turk's shaggy coat was soon saturated and he began to feel very wet and miserable. Then he ran out of the belt of rain and the ground was dry again. He smelt the smoke of a wood fire. There, half a mile away, the smoke was rising in thin blue clouds beside a wood. Turk knew well that where there was a fire, there was usually food and shelter and the company of man.

He scampered down the hill. There by a thick tree trunk, was a fire. The embers glowed red and a man in a tattered coat was feeding it with thick twigs that crackled and sparked as they caught alight. Perched on the embers was a battered tin can with a wire handle. In it something gave off a delicious smell. Turk drew closer. The man had his back to him. He turned to break up some more wood in a pile beside him and he saw Turk a couple of yards away, looking with wistful eyes at the can on the fire.

"Jings! We've got company!" the man exclaimed. He stood up and looked about him, peering among the bushes and looking as far up the moor as he could see in the gathering dusk, trying to see if there was anyone with the dog. Turk stood, lifting first one forefoot and then the other, uncertain of his welcome.

"Are you alone then?" the man asked him.

The man had not lifted a hand or a stick to drive him away and his voice sounded friendly. Turk advanced a yard nearer and stood looking at the man and wagging his tail.

"Friendly, aren't you?" the man said and put out his hand, palm up. "Come a bit closer then."

Cautiously Turk advanced, ready to jump away at the first unfriendly movement. The man held his hand quite still. Turk sniffed at it. It smelt of heather and bracken, of riverfish, rabbits and birds. It was engrained with the dirt of firemaking, but it was a clean kind of dirt to Turk, the smell of outdoors. When he had done sniffing he looked up at the man and wagged his tail again.

"Satisfied, are you?" the man laughed. He sat down again by the fire and Turk came nearer. The man patted the ground beside him. "Sit down," he said. Turk crouched down obediently beside the man and began to lick his paws.

"I wonder where *you've* come from?" the man said. "You've got burrs and bits of heather sticking to your coat and you're very wet and you're licking your feet as if they're tired and a bit sore. I guess you've strayed a long way from your home. Ah, well, maybe someone will come whistling for you soon. Meanwhile you're welcome to a share of my fire."

Turk knew the voice was friendly and he settled down even more comfortably by the fire, keeping an eye on the bubbling tin-can and every now and again giving a questioning sniff. The man stirred the contents. "Just about ready," he said, and took a tin plate out of the pack beside him. He ladled some of the meat out of the pan, the joints of a pheasant. Turk watched him put the meat in his mouth, the dog's eyes big with hunger. He could not refrain from giving a little whimper. The man looked at the saliva dripping from Turk's jaws.

"Hungry, are you? You've got manners too, for you don't pester me to give you a piece." He held out a pheasant's leg with the meat still attached to it. "Here you are, then."

Hungry as he was, Turk did not snatch at it but took it gently. The man gave him another piece when that was done, then he broke off a crust of bread from a small loaf and mopped up the gravy in the can and shared that with Turk too. "Not often I have a visitor," he remarked aloud. He produced a billycan from his pack, went to a small stream and filled it with water and made a brew of tea. When he had drunk half the contents of the can, he let it cool a little, then set it before Turk. "Your turn now," he said. "Share and share alike. Go on, dog!"

Turk looked at him questioningly, sniffed at the can, then put his nose inside and drank. When he had finished, the man washed the can in the stream, wiped it with a tuft of grass and restored it to his pack. The fire dropped low and the rain began again to patter through the leaves.

"Time we were looking for a shelter for the night," the man remarked. "Are you coming too, dog?" He rose and stamped out the dying embers. Turk stood up, too. "Come here, dog." The man held out his hand and this time Turk did not hesitate. He went to the man and sniffed his hand and gave it a lick. The man fondled his head and scratched him under his chin. "Nice friendly beast, aren't you? I wonder where you belong? Well, time we found somewhere to kip. Coming?"

The man picked up his pack and took a trail through the wood. Turk trotted beside him. They came to a country road going steeply downhill and reached farmlands on the fringe of a village. Here the man halted. "Quiet, dog!" he said. "No barking now! Here's where we've got to be careful. We don't want to rouse the farm dogs, so quiet!" He wagged a warning finger at Turk. Turk *did* understand him. That was one of the things he had learned at the Peebles farm, when to bark and when *not* to bark. The word "Quiet!" had been part of his training. He slunk along at the heels of his new friend.

At a farm on the outskirts they came on a sheep-fold used for sheep-shearing. There was a small hut where the farmer stacked his fleeces till he took them to the wool dealer. Turk knew all about sheep-folds and stacking sheds and he liked the familiar smell. His new friend tried the door of the shed. It was not locked for it was empty of fleeces. He pushed it open. The interior was gloomy and smelly but it was dry.

"Come on, dog. Here's a place for us," the man said. "I don't think anyone will know we're here if we keep quiet." He found two old sacks in a corner. "Bedding provided too!" he chuckled. He lowered himself on to the sacks. "Come along, dog. Lie down!" he urged. Turk knew the words "Lie down!" He crouched beside his new friend and the man drew him closer. "We can keep each other warm, dog."

The man continued to talk to him in a low voice. "You're the first friend I've made since I took to the roads. I wasn't always a tramp, dog. Lost everything in a fire—wife, child, home. I was in hospital a long time. Folk said I'd gone queer in the head. Perhaps I had. I couldn't settle afterwards so I packed up and took to the roads. But why am I talking to you like this? You can't understand me, can you, old chap? And yet I'm not sure, for you look at me kindly as if you did. Maybe just talking to you helps, and I've never had anyone I could talk to quietly like this." The man's voice sank to a whisper as he stroked Turk's head. Turk snuggled closer to him as though he knew the man had need of comfort. Soon his head drooped over his paws and both man and dog slept.

The next morning Turk was awake with the first light. He went to the door and whined gently to go out. The man woke and opened the door for him and Turk disappeared into the dawn shadows. The man left the door open, thinking the dog might soon be back but when nearly half an hour went by he thought Turk had gone for good. A river ran near to the farm and the man went down to wash himself and to fill his billy-can. He spied Turk coming back along the river bank. The dog was carrying a wild duck in his jaws. He laid the bird at the tramp's feet, then looked up at him for praise.

"So you're a poacher too?" the man said. "Well, there's our dinner, anyway, and we've got to eat to live." He put the dead bird in his pack. "Well done, dog!"

The man knelt beside the river bank and began dabbling his fingers gently in the water. In the shadow under the bank a trout moved his tail-fin lazily with the current. Full of curiosity it came near to the moving fingers. The man tickled the trout on its underside and the trout seemed mesmerised by the gentle stroking. Turk watched with interest, his nose coming closer and closer to the water. Suddenly the man made a grab but the fish was too quick for him and darted a yard upstream. He was not quick enough for Turk, however. Turk made a leap and his jaws closed round the fish. He bounded out of the water again, then sat down at the man's feet and held up the fish in his mouth to him. The man took it from him and despatched the dazed fish with a stone. Turk gave a bark of satisfaction.

"So you've learned how to fish as well?" The man pushed the fish in his pack with the wild duck. "There's fish and meat for the day. Together we might make good partners, living off the land," the man laughed. It was the first time he had laughed for a long time. "We'd better move on now, if we don't want to be arrested for poaching. Coming my way, chum? I want to go to Scotland." He pointed to the north. "Is that the way you want to go, too?"

They forded the river at a shallow point, jumping from stone to stone. Turk sniffed the breeze and caught the smell of the heather and sheep once more. Together they left the fields behind and headed for the open moors.

Their partnership was to last for more than a month. They did indeed live off the land; rabbits, wild-fowl, fish, and the man occasionally bought bread and a couple of eggs when they came to a village. Sometimes, under cover of night, he lifted a turnip or potatoes from a field. These he added to their stew. He shared everything with Turk and when Turk went poaching he faithfully brought everything to the man.

"I wonder if you've adopted me or whether I've adopted you, chum," the man said. "I'd hate to part with you now." He talked often to the dog at night and his heart was the easier for it. Turk listened to him with his head on one side. Turk had not been so happy for a long time either. This was something like the companionship he had had with old David Murray, though the understanding was not so close.

Day by day they pushed on northward towards the Border Hills. At night they slept in barns, under haystacks, in tumble-down deserted cottages, anywhere that gave them shelter, huddled together against the cold. The days grew shorter and the nights longer. Food was harder to get and the man's small store of money was nearly finished. Sometimes they had only bread and water between them. Both man and dog grew thinner but still they pressed on, both towards their secret goals.

The heather had turned black and the grass was often slippery with frost. It was late November and the distant hills had a light covering of snow. Still they struggled on, though the man's strength grew less each day. Once Turk flushed a grouse on the moor and that good meat helped them a little. They woke one morning in a stone sheep-fank and found the ground hard with frost and a thick mist hiding the landscape.

"We'll have to leave the hills now, chum, and take the

roads between town and town," the man said. "If we stay on the hills in these mists we could go round in circles for days."

They were only able to see a few yards in front of them as they went downhill. The mist whirled about them in strange ghostly shapes. They could only guess their way. Turk went ahead and the man followed slowly, a strange pain at his chest. There were no sheep on the hills now. They were all gathered in the fields near the farms but Turk could smell them afar off and he knew their way must lead to the farms. He followed the scent down into the valley.

All at once the land fell away down a steep slope to a small quarry. The grass was slippery with frost. They came on the sharp descent too soon and neither man nor dog could stop themselves from sliding over the edge of a small cliff into the quarry below. Turk landed lightly on his four feet but the man fell heavily against a large quarried stone, his leg bent under him. There was a sharp crack and the man fainted with the shock. Turk licked his face anxiously and the man came to and tried to stand but his broken leg gave way under him. The perspiration stood out on his forehead with the pain.

"It's no good, chum. I can't walk," he gasped.

Turk moved anxiously from one paw to the other, watching him. He knew something was badly wrong. The man shook his head at him.

"I can't get up, old chap," he said. Pain, exhaustion and hunger were too much for him and he slipped once more into unconsciousness. Turk licked his face and hands but the man did not open his eyes again. Turk barked loudly to try to summon help, but no help came. Turk knew that he would have to go out on the road and *find* someone to help the man. He must find *people*. He went running on to the road barking loudly, imploringly.

The road was empty but in the distance, through the fog, Turk could hear the lowing of cattle. The cows would be in the byre when it was hard frost, and a byre would be close to a farm. At a farm there would be people. He set off at a quick run towards the farm.

Just before he got there he came to a haystack at the edge of a field. There were two men there with a farm wagon. One was cutting slices of the hay with a hay-knife, a big spade-like tool, while the other was lifting the sections of hay with a fork on to the wagon. They were carting winter feed to the cows at the farm. Turk ran into the field and barked up at the men, sharp demanding barks to get their attention. The man stopped cutting the hay.

"Whose dog is that, Jock? He's not yours, is he?"

"No, Andrew. He looks like a lost sheep-dog but I haven't heard of anyone round here who's missing a collie."

Turk continued to bark at them, run a few steps towards the road, then back to bark at them again.

"Seems like he's trying to tell us something," Jock said, jumping down from the haystack. He held out a hand to Turk. "What is it, old chap?"

Turk ran again to the road, then back to them once more and stood barking. The two men went towards him and immediately he ran to the road and stood there waiting for them.

"He looks as if he's wanting us to follow him," Andrew said.

"Aye, they're intelligent animals, sheep-dogs. Perhaps there's a sheep in trouble somewhere. Let's go up the road and see what he's after."

As soon as they began to walk along the road Turk ran ahead a bit, came back, and jumped about their feet. He kept repeating these actions, watching them anxiously to make sure they were following him.

"He's leading us somewhere, that's for certain," Jock declared.

They followed the dog along the road for a couple of hundred yards. The mist was thinning. Suddenly Turk swerved left.

"He's gone into the old quarry!" Jock exclaimed.

Turk rushed up to his friend, still lying unconscious, then back again to the entrance. It was all right: the men were coming after him into the quarry. They started running when they saw the man lying on the ground. Jock bent over him and thrust a hand inside the man's shirt.

"Is he dead?" Andrew asked.

"No, he's breathing, but he's in a bad way. Looks like he's had a nasty fall into the quarry. He's got a leg twisted and bent under him, but there's more to it than a fall, I'm thinking. He's as thin as a rail and blue with cold. We'll have to get the poor chap into hospital. Run to the farm, Andrew, and ask my mother to phone for a doctor and an ambulance. It would be as well if she called the police too, in case the chap dies. I don't like the way he's breathing. I'll stay here beside him. Bring a couple of blankets back with you."

Andrew rushed away and Jock stripped off his tweed jacket and laid it over the man and tried to lift him into a more comfortable position. The man stirred and opened his eyes.

"It's all right," Jock told him. "We'll soon have you fixed up. My mate has gone to phone for a doctor."

The man closed his eyes and appeared to drift back into unconsciousness again, then suddenly he spoke. "The dog?" he said, opening his eyes wide.

"He's here beside you. He brought us to you," Jock told him.

"Good dog!" the man whispered. "Where are you chum?"

Turk came and licked his cold hands.

Soon Andrew was back at the quarry on the farm wagon, bringing blankets with him. They wrapped the man in them and Turk crouched close to his friend as if to lend him warmth.

"You're a clever faithful beast, aren't you?" Jock stooped to pat him. "It seems strange for a kind of tramp to have a dog like you."

Soon a car and an ambulance turned into the quarry. A doctor jumped out of the car. He made a quick examination of the injured man. "A broken leg and extensive bruising, but I'd say the main trouble is exhaustion and apparent starvation." He listened to the man's breathing. "There's some chest trouble too, pneumonia possibly. Get him on to the stretcher and into the ambulance."

Gentle hands heaped the blankets about the man on the stretcher. Just as he was being lifted into the ambulance a police-van drove up. The police asked a few rapid questions.

"Do you know who he is, Doctor Munro?"

The doctor shook his head. "Just a tramp, I guess. Jock Stevens found him here a short while ago."

"Aye, his dog came to the stack-yard and brought us here."

"His dog?"

Jock pointed to Turk who was trying to get into the ambulance beside his friend. An ambulance man lifted him out again. "You can't go in there, dog." He turned to the police. "You'll have to do something about the dog. I can't take him to the hospital."

The men closed the doors of the ambulance with Turk leaping up and down frantically outside them. The ambulance was being driven away and Turk began to run after it. A policeman caught him by the collar and tried to soothe him. "It's all right, dog. You can come with us." He lifted the dog into the back of the police-van. "We'll find a place for you till your master comes out of hospital." The police-van rattled out of the quarry. From inside the van Turk barked and whined sadly.

"Well, the fellow may only have been a tramp but the dog thought a lot of him," Jock Stevens remarked.

When the doors of the police-van were opened at the station at Hexham the policeman put a restraining hand on Turk's collar. "This way, lad! We shan't hurt you," he said, and led him inside. The station sergeant peered in surprise over the counter.

"What you got there, Joe?"

"Well, I suppose you might call him a vagrant."

"He's not been harrying sheep, has he?"

"Oh, no! I reckon he's a good dog." The policeman told the sergeant the circumstances under which he had found Turk.

"He looks a good-bred Border collie. It's queer a tramp having a dog like that. He's wearing a collar. What's the name on it?"

"That's another queer thing. There's no name on the metal tab."

"I'll just have to enter him in the books as 'Dog, found with tramp in quarry, names unknown'," Sergeant Duff decided.

"I think the poor beast might be hungry, if the man's condition is anything to go by. Got anything we can give him to eat?" the constable asked.

"There was minced steak in the canteen for dinner. Maybe

it wasn't all eaten up. See if you can rustle some up, there's a good lad," the sergeant told the police cadet at his elbow.

"Bring the dog a bowl of water too. He'll be thirsty as well," the constable suggested.

The cadet brought the meat and Turk set to work on it with an appetite sharpened by semi-starvation. The three men watched him eat.

"What'll happen to him now?" the cadet asked.

Sergeant Duff scratched his head with his pen. "That's a bit of a poser. He's not exactly a *lost* dog but I'd imagine that poor tramp in hospital won't be able to claim him for a long time to come, if ever he does get out of hospital, from what you tell me, Joe."

"The dog seemed very attached to him," Joe remarked.

"Aye, but that doesn't prove ownership."

"What'll we do with him, then?"

"We can't keep him at the police-station indefinitely. He'll have to go to a home for lost dogs," Sergeant Duff decided.

"And what'll happen to him there?" the cadet wanted to know.

"Someone might come along who wanted to adopt him. They like to find good homes for their lost dogs."

"But he's *not* lost, not while that chap's in hospital," Constable Joe insisted.

"Aye, I grant you've a point there, Joe, but something will have to be arranged for the dog. I think the Dogs' Home will take him till it's decided by a magistrate what's to be done with him." The sergeant lifted the telephone and dialled a number and talked briskly into the phone. He finished by saying, "Right, madam, we'll manage to keep the dog here till tomorrow."

"Bit of difficulty, Sergeant?" Joe asked.

"Aye, Joe. Mr Ford's away in Newcastle and Mrs Ford says she can't take in any more dogs without her husband's authority. She thinks he might manage to make room for the dog tomorrow, though, when he gets back."

"What'll we do with him in the meantime?" Joe asked.

"He'll have to stay here, I suppose, but we can't have him wandering round in front of the station, not with folk coming in and out. He'll be all right in one of the cells, they're centrally heated. Number Three is empty just now. Put him in there."

Joe led Turk by the collar to the cell, patted him and said, "Good dog! Lie down!" Turk obeyed him. "Good dog! When I'm off duty I'll come and take you for a walk."

At the word "walk" Turk looked up eagerly, but the door closed behind his policeman friend. Turk explored the room after he had gone, sniffing around the chair and the bed. There was no scent like any he knew; merely a strong antiseptic smell of soap. He sniffed at the foot of the door. He was troubled that his friend the tramp had been taken from him. He felt it was his duty to find him again. The cell was empty and lonely and the walls seemed to close in on him. He gave a sad little whine. No one came. He whined again, louder this time. Nothing happened. He put his head back and howled in loneliness and grief. Then, when the door still remained shut, he lay down in despair. The cell was warm and his stomach was lined with the good food he had been given and he fell asleep.

When he wakened he was still alone and the door shut. He went to the door, put his ear down to the foot of it and listened. In the outer office there was a rustle of paper as the sergeant wrote his reports. He was the sergeant on duty overnight, not the one who had received Turk. Turk heard the rustle and whined to attract attention. The sergeant paid no heed. Turk whined again, then howled. Still no one came. Turk began to bark, loudly and incessantly. He was mad to get out of the narrow place in which he was imprisoned.

Then, in desperation, he scratched at the door, a thing he had never done before in his life, barking all the time.

This time the duty sergeant heard him and irately left the outer office. He flung the door of the cell open. Turk was waiting just behind it and rushed past the sergeant into the outer office. Just at that moment the street door opened and another policeman came in to report for duty. Turk seized his chance, rushed between the policeman's legs, almost knocking him off his balance, and out into the street.

"Mercy me! What was that?" the policeman gasped.

"Och! Some stray brute that Joe brought in yesterday. Just go and take a look along the street and bring him back. He can't have gone far and I'll have to account for him."

Shortly afterwards Constable Lowe returned and reported there was no sign of the dog anywhere.

"Ah, well, someone's sure to find him and bring him to the station," the sergeant remarked casually. "He'll turn up somewhere when he wants food. Dogs always do."

But Turk did not turn up at the police-station again. As soon as he was free he bolted through the dark streets, quiet now of traffic, and took to the fields. He found his way by scent and instinct to the quarry where his friend had lain before he was taken away in the ambulance, but there the scent failed. Turk sniffed around, trying to pick up the trail but it was in vain. His friend had vanished utterly. Turk was at a loss for a few minutes, then instinct urged him to go northwards again, with a hope of finding the man on the moors. He left a network of narrow lanes behind him and pressed on, crossing a river by a footbridge. Now he was north of the Tyne. At Low Brunton the land grew steeper with the hills on each side beginning to slope towards the river valley. Turk stopped a moment to smell the message of the moors. He found himself running along the base of a low broken wall, topping a slope that rose higher to the crest of a hill. He had gone nearly three miles when a gap occurred in the square stones of the wall. Turk paused and looked through it. He did not know that he was standing where many a Roman soldier had stood on sentry-go centuries before. That meant nothing to Turk, but as he stood in the gap he quivered with joy. The country fell away steeply below him to farm-lands jewelled with small lakes that reflected the blue of the sky. The land rose again by rolling hills to rocky crags that cut a fretted ridge against the pale sky of late November. The moors dipped and rose in a thousand folds to the high fells of Hopehouse, Caplestone and Larriston. They were furrowed by a thousand mountain streams rushing to unite in a larger river.

Turk widened his nostrils to the delicious scents that came to him from the moorlands; of heather and furze-bushes; of peat and wood-smoke; of sheep and farms. The cold north wind brought with it the scent of the Border Hills, the particular scent of *home* to Turk. Now he knew for certain that he was headed the way he wanted to go. With the breath of the north country there came to him the memory of the man whom he had loved to the depth of his being, his old master at Glenbield. Somehow he *must* get back to Glenbield, for there were others he loved there too. There, over those steep fells and crags lay the way that he must go. He hesitated no longer but plunged downwards through the farm-lands and breasted the foot-hills that led to the moors. Not till he found himself among the blackened roots of heather did he come to a halt.

When night drew on he found a sheltered hollow and cowered low among the heather roots. Though he shivered with the cold, his shaggy coat protected him and he slept. He was hungry in the morning for he had missed his evening meal, but to be hungry for *one* day does not distress a sheep-dog too much. It was colder when he woke from his uneasy sleep. Ice had formed on the edge of the stream that trickled down the hillside and Turk had to break it with his paw before he could drink. Food there was none. He set off across the moors again but the going was harder than on the previous day. The moorland pools were iced over and the tufted grass was hard and brittle against his pads. The skies were sullen and grey with unshed snow. Still he ran on ever northwards.

Darkness came down early and the night was without stars. Turk found a little cave in a hill-side. Some hill walkers must have camped there in the summer for there were the sodden ashes of a wood fire just at the entrance to the cave and inside was a pile of faded bracken, cold but dry. Turk scrabbled with his paws among it, turned round a few times and then lay down. He licked his sore pads and curled up to sleep. This was the second night he had lain down supperless. Hunger was beginning to gnaw at him.

In the morning he woke to find a film of snow lying white over the moor. No sheep-dog fears snow. They are too accustomed to searching for sheep beneath the snow drifts. He set off across the white moors. The snow made the going softer to his sore pads but he was slower for occasionally he had to smell his way to be sure he did not fall into holes. The hunger in him grew like a sharp pain. He knew he must eat soon or die. Small animals were invisible under the snow blanket. They could stay there for days without leaving their lairs or borrows. Once or twice Turk scratched the snow away from their likely hiding-places, but he was always unlucky and the hiding-place was empty. The skies grew more louring with promise of heavier falls of snow. Turk sensed the oncoming snowstorm and he knew he would have to leave the hills and go down to the haunts of man if he hoped to find food.

He came down the hill to a farm on the outskirts of a

village. He approached it cautiously for he knew how jealously farm dogs guarded their territory. He sniffed round, coming a few feet nearer every time till he was on the edge of the farmyard. He was lucky. The farmer was out with his shepherd to bring his sheep down to the field next to the farm where he could feed them on turnip. He had taken his dogs with him. Turk gave one sharp enquiring bark and when there was no answering growl he knew there was no dog in the yard. Still he waited, crouched in the hedge.

A woman opened the door and called "Puss! Puss!" and a sleek black cat appeared from a barn. Beside the door she set down a saucer of milk for the cat and some pieces of fish. Turk waited till the door was closed, then he beat the cat in a race for the milk and food. She flew at him spitting and yowling but backed away when he curled back his lip at her and showed his teeth. He bent his head to the saucer and lapped quickly and furiously, keeping an eye on the cat. She watched him with yellow, angry eyes. He seized a piece of fish and then she flew at him with claws outstretched, letting out a howl of rage. Turk leaped in the air, still holding the fish in his mouth, and dodged her fiendish claws but he upset the saucer with a clatter. The clatter and the noise outside brought the farmer's wife to the door. At a glance she took in what was happening. A strange dog at the cat's food! "Away, you!" she shouted and made a swipe at Turk with her dish-cloth.

Turk knew better than to take on an angry woman as well as an angry cat and he bolted out of the farmyard, still with the fish in his mouth. He did not retreat far, however. As soon as he was out of sight behind the barn he devoured the fish as fast as he could, keeping his ears cocked all the time. He heard the farm dogs coming back to the farm and he ran as fast as he could away from the farm and towards the hills again.

The milk and the fish had given him new strength. This time, however, he did not take to the heights but kept to the foot-hills for he knew that when the snow came it would be heavy and sooner or later he would have to seek food at the valley farms. All that day he ran towards the north, faltering a little as the afternoon drew on. Turk sniffed the air and knew the snow must come soon. He looked about him for a night's shelter but the foot-hills were desolate. He went towards the road. There was little traffic on it now because of the threat of the snow. He skirted a reservoir and ran along by the roadside, keeping close to the grassy verge. The road mounted and dipped again to the north. Soon it ran beside a river, the Jed Water. The snow began coming in flurries now and the darkness was closing in. One pad was very sore and Turk was beginning to limp. He came to a stretch of woodland with thick undergrowth and crept in among the trees. One tree was hollow at the foot. He crept into the protecting hollow. With the wood to his back he felt safe and he slept the sleep of utter exhaustion.

When he awoke even the trees were white-armed skeletons and a drift of snow had built up against the hollow tree, almost shutting him in. He scraped it away with his paws and floundered out, sinking up to his stomach in the drifts. He gained the road with difficulty. Here, too, the wind had drifted the snow but it had left patches of the road bare so he was able to make his way along it, pushing through the drifts from one patch to the next. Luckily the road led north. Once again he felt very hungry. He reached a farm and crept towards the door, sliding over the snow on his stomach. The loud barking of the farm dog inside the house stopped him. He was scrabbling in the snow to get a firm footing to turn round again when his paw touched something hard. He sniffed at it, then set to work to scrape round it, delicately. It was an egg that a hen had laid away instead of in the poultry house. Turk took it gently in his jaws. Here was food. He turned away from the farm and found a sheltered corner by a haystack. Here he carefully cracked the egg so that the contents remained in the shell and he could suck them out.

There was more barking from the farm and Turk followed his own tracks back to the road again and plodded on north-wards. He went through a maze of lanes among the farm-lands. All that day he pushed west and steadily north but more slowly because of his sore feet and the drifts of snow.

It was well into the afternoon when he crossed the shoulder of a hill and looked down into a river valley below. His heart gave a leap of joy. There below him was a river that he knew. It was the Yarrow Water. That was where some of the film of *Flash the Sheep-Dog* had been made. That was where old David Murray had directed him from behind the film camera. That was where the camera crew and the actors had made much of him. The spark of memory kindled in him the urge to push on, tired, starved and weak as he was. Beyond that river lay the way home. From there he could find his remembered way. He gave a sharp bark of recognition and raced down the hill, sometimes rolling over on the snowy slopes in his eagerness.

When he reached the river bank he did not hesitate but plunged straight into the water. He gave a sharp gasp. The water was icy cold and in spate from the snow-fall on the surrounding hills. He swam hard in his dog-paddle, trying to strike out towards the opposite bank, but the current carried him along. He managed to keep his head above the fast-flowing stream but he was banged and bruised among the rocks. He tried to scramble on to a rock in mid-stream but his paws could not get a grip on the icy side and the current tore him away again. Then, just when Turk was despairing and half-drowned, the current swept him into an eddy under the north bank where a fallen tree overhung the water. Turk found himself pressed up against a branch. He managed to get his fore-paws up and around it and to pull his head out of the water so he could breathe. When he had got his breath back he dug in his claws and pulled himself further along the

branch till he reached the tree-trunk. This time he was slow and cautious. He did not want to fall into the river again. Soaked, cold and terrified, he crept along the trunk until he was able to bound safely on to the bank.

The river had carried him half a mile downstream where the Whitehope Burn runs to join the Yarrow Water. All along the valley the country road follows the river. Dusk was already falling when Turk struggled ashore and along the road. His strength was giving out and he was nigh dead with cold. The frost was so keen that it had already frozen the water into tiny icicles at the ends of the hairs of his coat. He still had to find shelter and food. If he did not, he knew he might well be dead by morning.

In the fast-growing dark he dragged himself along the road, till he came to a right-angled bend close by a bridge over the river. There he came to an abrupt stop. Before him there winked a number of red lights. They came from lamps set there by road-repairers to guard a long hole they had dug in the road. On the verge of the repairs was a watchman's hut and before it glowed a coke fire in a brazier. The watchman was sitting in his hut, holding out his hands to the fire and thinking about his evening meal.

Turk crept up to the opposite side of the brazier. The watchman saw the slinking shadow and cried out "What's there?" and reached for his stick in the hut behind him. Luckily he saw Turk before he used it. "Why! It's a sheep-dog!" he exclaimed. "What are you doing here on a night like this? You must be from some farm hereabouts."

Turk was encouraged by his voice to come nearer to the fire.

"Come here and let me look at you," the man said, holding out his hand. Turk sniffed at the outstretched hand but he did not go too close. He was wary of strangers who might put a rope or a leash round his neck. The warmth of the brazier was tempting, though, and he ventured a little nearer the fire.

"Mighty me, lad, you're frozen!" the watchman exclaimed, seeing the icicles on Turk's coat. "Have you been in the river? Get down by the fire, dog, and dry yourself. Down, now!"

Turk understood. He lay down on his stomach beside the brazier and felt the comforting heat on his coat. The icicles began to thaw and the water to drip from him. He kept a steady eye on the watchman, though.

The watchman felt under the seat in the hut and produced a kettle of water which he balanced on the brazier. "We'll make a drop of tea, lad," he told Turk. While the water was heating he produced tea and sugar in a tea-pot and from a carrier-bag some slices of bread and links of sausage. Turk edged a little nearer, feeling the saliva gather in his mouth.

The watchman made toast on a fork. He cut off a crust and threw it to Turk who snatched it up quickly. Then the watchman held a sausage over the red-hot coke till it browned and sizzled, clapped it on the toast and ate it. Turk sat up, watching him with wistful eyes. When the last vestige of sausage disappeared Turk gave a sad whine. The watchman looked at him. "Are ye hungry, dog?" he asked. He saw Turk's painfully thin ribs for now his coat had thawed and the water held it sleek against the dog's body. "Could you be doing with a sausage?"

This time he impaled two sausages on the prongs of the fork and held them over the brazier. Turk's eyes never left the sausages all the time they were toasting. When they were done, the watchman made a sandwich again of one of them, but he tossed the other to Turk. Turk caught it in mid-air but he quickly dropped it again before it burned his mouth. It was too hot for him to eat but he nosed it over and over in the snow till it cooled down. Then he gobbled it in a couple of bites.

The watchman sat back and laughed. "You're as good as an entertainment, dog!" he told Turk. "Let's see if you'll do it again." Once more he toasted a couple of sausages over the brazier and Turk repeated the performance.

"A bit of company's nice on a lonely night," the watchman said. "I'll share my supper wi' ye, dog." He divided a cheese sandwich and gave Turk half of it and threw him a couple of biscuits. He made tea in the kettle and poured some into a mug for Turk and let it cool before he passed it to the dog.

Warmed and comforted Turk lay down beside the fire when the meal was done. This time he lay at the man's feet and in a while they both slept. During the night the watchman went the round of his lamps to make sure they were all burning, and Turk went with him. The man put another shovelful of coke on the brazier and they settled down to sleep again.

With the coming of daylight the man stirred purposefully, brewed tea again and this time toasted two slices of bacon over the fire. He threw a third slice of bacon to Turk, but this time it was raw, for the man had no time for entertainment before the roadmen appeared. He went along the row of lamps, extinguishing them, then carried them to his hut to store them there till next evening.

"Off with you now, dog! Back home!" he said, giving Turk a friendly pat. "Some farmer'll be missing you."

Turk knew he was being told to go. He set off on the narrow hill road by the Whitehope Burn. As he skirted Welshie Law the snow began to fall again, not in short showers now but thickly and incessantly. The landscape was a blur and Turk made his way very slowly by Glengaber to the Fingland Burn. He had to fight his way along against the driving wind. Time and again he fell into a deep snow-drift

Turk's Long Journey —
south-west to Wigan, and north again to the hills of home

and floundered about in it till he got out again. At last the
Fingland Burn brought him to Traquair. It had taken him
almost five hours to cover the five miles from Yarrow to
Traquair where the stream ran into the Tweed. This was
country well known to Turk for he had often come among
the Tweedside farms with his master when they had been
buying or selling sheep. He knew he was on the last lap of his
journey. But he knew too that he would soon have to cross
the wide River Tweed.

The Tweed was running very fast indeed, in full spate, the
water brown from the peat of the hill burns in flood. Turk
eyed it. He knew that this time he dare not risk swimming
across it. It was running far too fast and too deep and it
would be bitterly cold. He had learned a lesson from his
experience in the Yarrow Water. This time he would have to
seek a bridge. He turned left along the road that lay on the
south bank of the river. He faced into the driving snow and
pushed his way along. Very little traffic came along this road
except in summer. Most traffic took the wider road on the
north bank of the river. There had been few cars or vans to
flatten the snow which at times reached to Turk's chest. His
progress became slower still. He could only push on a yard or
two at a time, pushing the snow in front of him with his chest.
Darkness had fallen by the time he was within a couple of
miles of the town of Peebles but here the road was wider and
had been more used earlier in the day. Turk skidded along
the tracks where a van had passed and hardened the snow
into ruts. There was no traffic now. Indeed, Turk came on an
abandoned car, snow up to the hub-caps and sheeted in
white. Still Turk fought the snow-drifts and floundered on his
way till he came to a place where a snow-plough had swept
one side of the road. He had reached the wide old bridge of
Peebles spanning the Tweed. Turk rounded a corner and
found himself in the fine broad High Street. It was a deserted

street now. The pavements had been cleared during the day but already the new falling snow had carpeted them. The shops were closed and the folk of Peebles were indoors, their feet at their fires and the curtains close-drawn against the bitter weather. Few strayed abroad on a night like this with a high wind and drifting snow.

Turk ran along the High Street, past the old Tontine and Cross-Keys inns where he had sometimes been with David Murray on market days, for a meal with other farmers. He recognised his surroundings with joy though he could hardly drag himself along for weariness. No need to nose about now to get his bearings! He turned up Northgate and crossed the bridge to the Edinburgh road. He still had more than a formidable mile before him, one of the toughest parts of the whole journey.

He took a road on the right which wound uphill over a stony way. Drifts were piled up at the gates which crossed it. He had to scratch his way through them like a rabbit burrowing. The road grew steeper and steeper, winding along the edge of a precipice above the Soonhope Burn. Turk could hear the stream rushing along far away below him, but to him it sounded like a welcome home. The leg that had been broken ached badly and sometimes he limped on three legs to ease it. He felt as if his legs would take him no further and he sank down in the snow. As he lay there, the snow began to settle on him. Sleep began to overcome him. Then Turk heard a sound from the farm byre in the next dip of the road and it roused him to make yet one more effort. Half-limping, half-dragging himself on his stomach, he reached the steep bank above the farmyard. Here the snow had been cleared to make a path to the byre. Turk slithered over the slippery cobbles and with a thud landed in a heap at the farm-house door. He was too weak to bark and could only give a feeble whine.

In the farm-house the Murray family had just gathered round the blazing fire after clearing away the evening meal. Lil, the Border collie bitch who was Turk's mother, was sitting in a corner by the fire. The Murrays had always loved their dogs as part of the family and on a bitter night like this, made sure they were safe and warm indoors. Lil was restless and kept pricking up her ears.

"What ails Lil?" Ann asked. "She can't seem to settle tonight."

"It'll be the storm outside," her father said. "It aye makes the beasts restless."

"She seems to be listening all the time," Mrs Murray remarked.

Garry, too, seemed fidgety. There was a dull thud against the door leading to the farmyard. Both dogs gave a quick bark.

"Quiet!" David Murray told them. "It'll likely just be the snow falling off the roof. A wind like yon would bring it off."

There was a feeble whine outside but the family could not hear it above the wind. The dogs heard it, though, and both started up and went to the door.

"There must be something or someone in the farmyard," Mrs Murray declared.

"It might be a fox," David Murray said. "The bitter weather drives them down from the hills. I'll go make certain all the hens and ducks are safely penned."

He opened the outer door, and the snow blew into his face in such a flurry that it almost blinded him and he nearly fell over the crumpled inert body on the doorstep. The other dogs barked shrilly.

"Mercy me! What's here?" he exclaimed, stooping over Turk and brushing the snow off him. "Heavens above! It canna' be! No! Yes, yes, it *is*!" His voice rose a pitch higher with excitement and joy. "It *is*, it's *Turk*!"

The whole family jumped from their chairs and rushed to the door. "Turk? Turk come back? It can't be!"

David Murray lifted Turk in his arms and carried him to the fire. "My! He's that *light*. He's just a rickle of bones. He's in a poor way." He looked concerned.

Turk tried to give a feeble wag of his tail.

"He's nigh dying of hunger and cold," David said, his voice full of pity.

"Oh, no! He hasn't come back to *die*, has he?" Ann almost burst into tears.

"I'll get some warm milk into him," Mrs Murray said, hurriedly filling a pan and putting it on the stove.

"Lace it with a drop of brandy from the cupboard," David told her. The brandy was kept by in case of an emergency with the sheep.

In a few minutes Mrs Murray had the warm milk and brandy in a bowl. David still held Turk in his arms. He set him down on the hearthrug with the bowl before him. Turk could hardly stand up to drink. "Put a drop in a saucer," David suggested. "He canna lift his head to get it in the bowl."

Turk managed little better with the saucer, then Ann had a brilliant idea. "Let's try the baby's bottle that we feed the lambs with when they've got no mothers."

The bottle was brought and Ann eased it between Turk's swollen gums. He licked his tongue round it and then began to suck. Ann gave him the milk a few pulls at a time. Turk felt the warmth and new life throbbing through his veins. "He's getting stronger. He's *pulling* at the bottle now," Ann whispered. The level of the milk in the bottle began to go down quickly, then, in triumph, Ann held up the empty bottle. "He's finished it. Shall we give him another?"

"Not just yet. We'll have to feed him little by little. If we give him too much at once it'll just make him sick," her father warned her. "We'll give him some more in about half an hour."

"He's still shivering," Helen remarked.

Mrs Murray seized the rug that was lying across the settee, warmed it and wrapped it round him. "I wonder where he's been all this time?" she said.

David Murray examined Turk gently. "He looks to have had a broken leg some time. His pads are cracked and bleeding, too. He must have come a terrible long way."

"He must have loved us a lot to endure so much to get back to us," Mrs Murray declared.

"Will he ever be able to drive the sheep again, Father?" Helen asked.

"Aye, lassie, after a good long rest and plenty of good food, but he'll never be as fast as he was. I doubt if he'll ever be good enough to take part in the Sheep-Dog Trials again, but that doesn't matter so long as we have him home again."

"He's still *beautiful*," Ann declared.

"I think Grandpa would be happy to know that he was back," Helen said quietly, kneeling on the rug and encircling him with her arms.

Turk opened his eyes and lifted his head. He looked straight towards the chair where Grandpa used to sit, then his gaze wandered round the circle of kindly faces and he knew that these were *his* people, that he belonged to them and they belonged to him, just as he and Grandpa had belonged to each other. His spirit was healed and he had indeed come home.

CATCH A KELPIE

If you enjoyed this book
you would probably enjoy our other Kelpies.

Here's a complete list to choose from: